Ace

by Heather B

Copyrights

Chapter 1: Joanie

I've fucked up now. I'm sitting in the living room of my parents' house. Mom and my uncle Cowboy are having a conversation about where I was at when he found me earlier tonight. No one has asked me why I was there.

I left here Thursday afternoon under the guise of doing my homeschooling with a friend the next day, and then we were going to see a movie after school. My mom is usually a bit lax on mine and my brother Liam's homeschooling on Fridays, since we don't have any class connects. Class connects are virtual classes with our teachers for our core classes, such as math and English. As long as we get our work done, we are golden.

When mom dropped me off at Jen's house shortly before four, we waited a few minutes before we left in Jen's car and went to the Navy recruiting office. I've been deciding on this for years. I want to follow in both my parents' footsteps being in the Navy. I've taken the ASVAB already and on Thursday evening, our recruiter drove us over to the MEPS hotel after reviewing our paperwork. Friday I went to MEPS. Jen is my buddy, she's enlisting too. Her parents know we're going to MEPS, but I haven't told my parents. I feel like I know what they're going to say. They're going to say I'm making a rash decision because my brother got into the Navy and I just want to show him up. I don't. He got his choice job to be a SEAL, just like dad, only he enlisted instead of going the officer route. Me, I just want to figure out what to do with my life and I know the structure the military gives you will help keep me straight. It's time for me to step up and be an adult.

Either way, Friday was a disaster. We woke up and ate breakfast. Then the bus for MEPS showed up and we took it to the MEPS station. There must have been fifty other people heading with us to the MEPS station. The guys that run the MEPS station are our first taste of what it'll be like to be in boot camp. When we arrive, they lay out rules. We can't leave without signing out on the chart, smoking is allowed only in the gazebo, and whenever you are called you respond with yes sir, or moving sir.

Once the rules have been laid out, those that are shipping out that day are taken first into the medical area and then the rest of us are led into a classroom. Our group has about halved since we loaded up at the hotel. There we filled out a million questions about our health. Most of the conditions they asked about I'd never heard of so, I selected no because if you've never heard of it you probably don't have it. Then I spot the two conditions that might seal my fate. I told the recruiter about them and he had said it would be up to the doctor. There was no way for me to hide them. Anyone who watches me for a prolonged period of time knows something isn't right with me. After paperwork, they lead us into a big waiting room where we are called individually by a nurse for our vitals, and then what seems like a million other physical tests. I pass those all with flying colors. I haven't touched drugs in two years, so I know I'm good on the drug test.

I wait nervously in the chairs waiting for my one on one with the doctor. I see Jen and even though we are not allowed to talk; we do. She and I have been talking the same way we did in school for years. We have a sort of sign language that we used over the cameras in class connects. She's nervous too. The doctor calls her before they call me, and I'm alone again. Not really alone, but my best friend isn't here with me anymore.

The cafeteria called for lunch earlier and I went to get something to eat, but now I'm really wishing I hadn't. Jen had finished her interview and was waiting to talk with the placement officer. We got to talk in the cafeteria for the short time we were there. They only gave us thirty minutes to go through the line and eat. Now that we're back in the main waiting room, I finally get called into the doctor's office. It's time for my one-on-one appointment. It's more of an interview than an examination. The doctor is an older man in his sixties or seventies. He flips through my papers and I see his eyebrows raise as he reads over my questionnaire.

He clears his throat and says, "ADHD and ODD?"

I can only nod at his question. I'm not lying. Hell, the MEPS officers have constantly told us the penalties for lying on the paperwork and it's enough to keep me from lying.

He then asks, "Do you take any medication for these conditions?"

My mouth feels dry but I manage to answer him, "No, sir. My mom tried me on medications when I was first diagnosed, but she didn't see any difference, so since they homeschooled me, she stopped giving them to me."

He nods and notes something in the medical chart. Then he asks, "How old were you when your parents stopped the medication?"

"Eight I think. Maybe younger." I answer. All my hopes to join the Navy lie in this mans hands and I'm nervous as hell.

He nods again and it's starting to irritate me. I want to scream at him to do something other than nod. I try to remember all my therapies and keep myself calm. He continues to look over my chart and finally flips back to the first page before grabbing one of two stamps off the desktop.

"Now young lady I'm doing this with your best interest at heart. You've got two neurological disorders, and I can see you're doing your best to control one of them right now. The other one is the concern. With your history of oppositional defiant disorder, I'm concerned about what you'll do when the training gets tough and you've got nowhere to go. I'm rejecting you from military service." His hand with the stamp comes down on the page with the word rejected in red stamps on my file.

I'm speechless for a moment. Then I start crying and babbling. I'm trying to ask a million questions at once.

"This isn't something you can get a waiver for, young lady." He says. He understood the questions I was trying to ask.

I get up and storm out of the office and into the main area of the MEPS station, saying a slew of curse words as I go. But my hell has only just begun. Since MEPS is close to home, I decide not to call my recruiter or to tell Jen. I just start walking. I'll eventually make it home. I follow the fifteen until I make it to the bay and then I head over towards the beach.

What I didn't realize was that when I didn't log into my classes on Friday by eleven in the morning, my mom got an alert from the school. I had to turn my phone off in the MEPS station, but the minute my phone powered on I had several missed calls from my mom. Now my phone is ringing. I look at the screen and guess who's calling; my mom. She probably thinks I've run away from home on one of my impulsive moments. But she's wrong. I was trying to make a lifetime decision and show her and my dad that ADHD and ODD didn't control me. I could control them.

I don't answer my phone. I keep walking along the boardwalk beside the ocean. Listening to the sounds of the waves crashing into the shore. Just as the sun sets, I hear a car slowing down beside me and then I hear my uncle Cowboy's southern draw say, "Joanie, get in."

I don't argue with any of my uncles. I hop into the car and although he tries to question me about where I was going; I don't answer him. I stay silent. My laptop is still at Jen's house. I'll worry about picking it and the rest of my weekend clothes up later, after I've had the major chewing out by my parents.

Only when I arrive home, it's just my mom. Dad has left for a few days on a trip to visit a friend. He apparently tore out this morning right after his pt session. It's not a mission that called him away, it's another SEAL. Someone named Viper, someone I've never met, but means a whole lot to my father.

Cowboy tries to calm my mom down telling her I was safe. He'd gone through the bag I had with me. It was just the overnight clothes, so he suggests I wasn't running away like my mom thinks. He hasn't told her about the military paperwork he found in the bag. He'd tried to question me about it, but I refused to answer him. It hurt too much at the moment. That damned doctor had torn my heart out. I wasn't even given a chance to prove myself and now my mom thinks I was just skipping school for the heck of it.

Mom doesn't even want my side of the story. She heads into the bedroom to call dad again. Apparently, when she couldn't get in touch with me earlier in the day, she called him. I know what she's going to tell him. Their derelict daughter has been found wandering the bay near Coronado. She's been saying she doesn't know what to do with me once I graduate high school this summer. Hell, my plan was blown out of the water. I had planned to come out of MEPS with a ship out date for boot camp of summer. I was going to show her when I came back from Jen's house on Sunday evening. Instead, I have nothing, no plans for the future. It's too late to apply to any of the local colleges. I don't even know what I want to do with my life. At least joining the military, I would have been given a job and trained to do it. Now I've got to see what I want to do and go from there.

God, I want a joint right now. I just want to quit feeling these feelings for a few hours. But two years ago, I promised my uncles I would quit experimenting with the drugs. I never tried anything hard. Just weed mostly. A couple of times I had tried some other things my friends had given me. Some prescription drugs they found you could get a quick high off of for a few hours. But that stuff never pulled me like it did them.

My knee bounces up and down as I try to control my anxiety. My phone rings and I look at it, It's Jen. Oh, goodness I didn't tell her I left. She's probably worried sick about me.

"Hello."

"Joanie where the fuck are you, girl?"

"Home."

"What? How did you get there?"

"Long story. Don't want to talk about it. Waiting for the judge to bring on my punishment."

"Oh shit. You got caught. Well, what do I tell Jack?"

"Permanently denied."

"Damn, girl. I'm sorry to hear that."

"How about you?"

"Ship out July 15th. I'm going to be a yeoman."

"Cool. Congrats girl. Gotta go, the judge is coming." I hang up the phone.

Mom pins me with one of her disappointed looks. She knew I was on the phone. She's probably going to take away all my privileges for phone and internet unless it is for school. Mom and Cowboy have another quiet conversation before she turns to me and says, "Joanie I'm disappointed in you. You and Jen lied to me. You abused my trust. When your dad gets back from Texas, we're going to have a sit down and decide how to handle you."

Great so now I've got to wait for the supreme leader to show his ass up before I know what my punishment is. Who knows how long that is going to be? I don't dare ask my mom that question. She'll take it as me being disrespectful. Instead, I ask, "Can I go to my room?"

"Yes." she says still in that disappointed tone.

I know without my mom saying it. I'm grounded to the house. I'm going to go to my room and try to chill out. As I leave the living room, I see my mom shoot my uncle Cowboy a confused look, but he doesn't betray me. I think he's figured out why I was out walking and why I am in the current mood.

I enter my room and turn up the radio. I'm going to just lay in my bed for a while and drown my sorrows in music and tears.

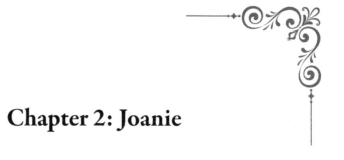

Chapter 2: Joanie

Dad finally comes home. He looks worn out. Mom and dad head into their room to 'talk'. They're deciding what to do with me since I made my latest fuck up.

Liam is with his recruiter at the base, so at least I don't have to worry about him chirping in with his two cents about my punishment. I had to go to a totally different recruiting office, so my parents didn't find out that I was talking to the recruiters.

Mom and I have been circling each other since the other day. She keeps telling me she loves me and is confused why I was walking around with only a day's change of clothes. I still refuse to answer her, it hurts too much to talk about.

While dad and mom are in their room, talking, Liam comes home. "So why did dad message me to come home for a family meeting?" He asks me as he heads to his room.

"I don't know." I answer him.

"You must have fucked up big this time." He muses.

"Shut up." I say, as I playfully slap my younger brother. He's smart, so smart he's going to graduate with me.

That's another of the annoying things I've got going on in my life. I can't even graduate a year ahead of my younger brother. He took opportunities I didn't and got extra credits allowing him practically to skip an entire grade, so at seventeen he'll be graduating. Plus, he's already gone to MEPS and has a ship out date and a contract. He's following in our dad's footsteps, sort of. He's going to be a SEAL, just not an officer. Dad tried to talk him into going to the academy and then to SEAL training, but Liam wants to start at the bottom. He's going to train to be a bomb expert or something like that, so he can be a benefit to the SEALs.

Mom and Dad come into the living room. Mom doesn't look happy, but dad, he's always been unreadable. What he says next sends my life into a tailspin.

"I've called a family discussion because things are about to change around here over the next week." Dad says.

"Why, dad?" Liam asks.

"I'm putting in my packet for retirement. I have accepted a job in Texas and my new employer is going to send some of his men to escort your mom and Joanie to their headquarters until my retirement is finalized." He informs us.

"Wait, dad what about me and my leaving for boot camp?" Liam is visibly nervous.

"I'm staying behind so you can finish high school and ship out for boot camp from here. I'm sending Annie and Joanie ahead of time for several reasons. First, my boss is building us a house on his property, and your mom, being there she can approve or deny the house ideas. Secondly, all the men are former SEALs and can help your mom keep an eye on Joanie. We think it will help Joanie by having a change of scenery." Dad explains.

Well this isn't so bad. I'm used to being surrounded by a group of SEALs. Then my dad says, "Joanie, you and your mom's escorts will be arriving in about three days. You'll have until then to pack your things. You can carry your school supplies and clothes that you'll need."

"What about my phone?" I ask, hoping I can keep in contact with my friends.

"Phone stays here." He answers, shooting my hopes down.

I look over to my mom and ask, "Can I at least see Jen before we leave?"

"No." It's a hard one word that comes from my dad.

I know not to argue with my dad. I nod in acknowledgement.

"Good. Now that we've got that ironed out, I need to check in on Viper." Dad says before he turns back to his and mom's bedroom.

I head to my room to pack for my punishment. Mom has had my phone since the other night. I decide I'll wash my clothes the day before we leave and I'll pick out most of my wears to pack now.

No one knows the pain I'm in at the moment. Every time I think of the Navy and what could have been, my heart clenches and I feel like there is no other pain like this. It's been my one dream since I first saw my uncles and my dad in their dress uniforms with all of the awards they had earned on thier chests. It's been my only love, no boy has ever touched my heart the way my want to join the military has. They just think that I made an impulsive move, but I'll keep that secret to myself.

I pull my suitcase out of my closet and throw it onto my bed. I unzip the lid and throw it open. Knowing that we're leaving in summer, I'm packing my summer clothes, not that I have a lot of winter clothes living in southern California. I first open my underwear drawer and as I'm packing, I'm going through my underwear. I guess it's mostly to make this take longer than it has to. I even grab two of my best swimsuits hoping there might be a pool to swim in, or mom might have a change of mind and let me leave the headquarters to go to a beach for a bit.

I hear the doorbell ring and I drop what I'm doing, hoping against hope that it's Jen. I bound down the hall, still not totally my normal self, but feeling better that Jen stopped by to visit me. Just as I'm approaching the living room, I see my mom closing the door. She's got my laptop and my overnight bag from Jen's mom. It's now obvious mom and Jen's mom have been in touch and I'm not allowed visitors.

Mom places my overnight bag on the couch for me to pick up and takes my laptop to their room. Yup, I'm grounded until further notice. I grab the overnight bag and head down the hall again. I've got clothes to pack.

Back in my room, I crank up my music and focus on finishing packing my underwear. Then I move on to the shorts and shirts. I don't really own much more than running shorts and tank tops. So I sort through them and pick the ones that are the best looking. Before I realize it, I've packed everything I'll need for my seclusion at this 'headquarters' aka my prison. Dad has promised he'll pack up the rest of our things and have them shipped closer to his retirement.

Chapter 3: Ace

I'm stuck on a two-day drive with Zeke, the geek, and Hawk. We're heading to California to pick up Viper's best friend's wife and daughter. It's a basic babysitting mission. No rifles needed, just our sidearms. This shouldn't be a dangerous mission, so we are all joking around as we head out to California. According to Zeke, who does all our gps of our trips, it'll take us almost a full day of driving without bathroom stops. He's mapped it and we'll spend a night in a hotel around Phoenix and drive the rest the second day. It makes the drive the easiest.

Viper and Ghost gave me a rundown of the daughter's issues. She's got ADHD and ODD. I'd never heard of the second one until Ghost told me about it. Apparently part of the autism spectrum it makes the person push their limits. They know the rules, but they push the limits to see what they can get away with. He and Annie have been struggling with Joanie her whole life. She can talk nonstop and then the anger and pushing her limits drive them to their breaking point. His men have tried their best to help them with her upbringing. It also explains her experimenting with drugs, although Ghost says he believes she hasn't touched drugs in a few years. I hope like hell he's right on the drugs part. Because if he's not and we transport her to Texas, she's going cold turkey and that's not fun on anyone.

Thankfully for my back, Hawk drove the suburban with its three rows of seating. There's plenty of leg room for my six-foot-two frame. I figure Annie and Joanie will sit in the backmost seat and me, Hawk, or Zeke, will sit in the middle row and the passenger seat while one drives.

The suburban even has lots of tailgate space, so it'll hold our three bags, my medical bag and whatever Annie and Joanie bring. I'm expecting them to bring everything but the kitchen sink. They're women and women pack for every potential event. Even if you tell them they're going to be gone a week, they'll pack three changes of clothes for the entire week. 'What if I get cold while we're in the store?' things. How do I know? I grew up with a single mom and two older sisters. So, now you know why I turned to the military and the most masculine part of the military I could find when I joined. I needed some real men to be around.

"We'll be at Ghost's house in about five minutes." Zeke calls out to us.

"Great, I really need to get out and stretch my back." I say in response to the five minute warning.

My back really hates long term sitting or standing. Too many jumps has killed my knees and lower back, it's part of the reason I hate these long rides and why I joined up with Viper and NRT. I can stay local if I need to, but he really needed a medic for this mission in case the daughter runs and gets her hands on drugs and overdoses.

We pull into a gravel driveway of a two-story house. Once Zeke shuts off the motor, I'm hopping out of the back bench seat to work the bench vice out of my back.

I'm walking around the expansive front yard when I see the young beauty. She's beautiful, just the first view I get of her, she's leaned up against the side of the house, lost in thought. She doesn't see me walking around in the yard, which gives me time to examine her more. Her hair is short and colored deep purple, and varying shades of blue and green. If I had to guess, she's a good five foot seven. Even from the distance I'm at, I can tell she's wearing a minimal amount of makeup. She's done her eyebrows in a similar shade of purple and the lipstick she's wearing is a shifting purple to green, the kind us guys like on show cars.

If this is Joanie, she's much different from what I'd imagined, and damn if she isn't beautiful. I'm going to have to keep my distance from this girl because she's everything I dream of in a woman. A decent set of breasts and an ass a man can grab a hold of, or maybe even give a good spanking to. *Shit, that thought just made my cock stir to life.* Maybe it's one of Joanie's friends, or even Liam's girlfriend. That would be a much better scenario, *at least for me.*

Zeke calls my name and I hurry over to where he's at. I need to get this woman out of my sight for the moment or else I might do something stupid and walk over there and plant a big claiming kiss on her beautiful lips.

Zeke introduces the team to Annie. Ghost is there with her, but we all know him. I notice there are only a few bags by the side door, and I'm wondering where the rest are.

"Is this everything the ladies are taking with them?" I ask, my interest piqued at the minimal amount of luggage.

"Yes. I'm going to bring the rest of the household when I finalize my retirement." Ghost answers. Placing a hand on Annie's shoulder.

"You understand we're going to search Joanie's luggage before we put it into the vehicle." I explain to the two parents. I know Ghost understands why, but I can see the shock on Annie's face. "Ma'am, it's only to make sure she's not bringing drugs or any of the items you and your husband have deemed off limits with her." I explain.

Annie finally nods and steps over to where Joanie's bag is. She picks it up and places it on the dining room table. "She's not allowed anything that can communicate with her friends, except for her laptop, which is used for her schoolwork." Annie explains. "She can have her tablet, it only connects to Wi-Fi for books and games. I don't want to take away her being able to play some of her games and reading books."

I nod at her statement as I unzip the bag she's identified as Joanie's. The easiest way to search it is to dump the contents out onto the table. As I dump the contents, I glance at them. Zeke comes over and grabs the two items Annie has said she's allowed to have that are electronics. He's going to put a tracker on her computer so we'll know the minute she reaches out to her friends through messaging apps.

Hawk and I make quick work of the girls' luggage, repacking it the way she had it as we go. We are about done when the side door to the house opens up and in steps the beauty I spotted earlier.

"What the fuck?" She roars at Ghost. "They're going through my clothes!"

"Joanie!" Ghost roars back at her. "It's part of the process. We don't want you carrying anything that will get you or them into trouble. No phones, nothing that can communicate with your friends, no drugs, and no cigarettes. They're just following protocol."

"I hate you! I wish I was never born." She yells as she storms down the hall and slams a door.

I look to Ghost, who nods for us to continue what we are doing. Hawk and I finish going through the one luggage and Annie hands us another bag. It's like a bookbag. There's a bunch of miscellaneous things in it. Mostly pens and such, but I must go through it. It's where her tablet was at. It must be her purse by the looks of the contents. Nothing stands out to me as dangerous. I put the items back into the bag and hand it back to Annie.

"Sorry about that. It's just one of her outbursts." Annie says as she takes the bag from my hand.

"It's okay. I grew up with older sisters. I'm used to hormonal outbursts." I reply, giving Annie a small smile.

"That was small compared to the normal outburst." Annie informs me.

Hawk and Zeke load the bags into the suburban. While I inform Ghost and Annie of our plans to head out the next morning. It's going to be exhausting for me, Zeke and Hawk, but the sooner we have Annie and Joanie at headquarters, the sooner Ghost will feel more at ease, hopefully.

"So, we'll let you guys say your goodbyes tonight. We're going to head out and grab some chow and check into a hotel to catch some sleep." I inform them.

"Why not stay here? We've got the space and it's free. Plus, no one beats Annie's home cooking. She makes enough for the whole base to eat, I swear," Ghost informs me.

"Oh, well, I guess we couldn't turn down home cooking and a decent bed to sleep in." I hear Hawk say as he and Zeke are returning from packing the suburban.

"Good, that's settled. I've got to make the garlic bread." Annie says breaking away from the conversation. "Joanie come help me set the table for dinner. We've got guests tonight!" Annie calls out as she makes her way into the kitchen.

I hear the teenager grumbling all the way into the kitchen. Ghost shows me, Zeke, and Hawk where we can bunk for the night. It's upstairs, where there's a large room that's been converted into a community bedroom. The adjoining room is Liam's, which he has a private half bath, and on the other side is another room, which Liam has transformed into a weight room. The community bedroom has several twin sized beds for guests. I'm assuming it's for Ghosts' team members' families when they come over.

We each toss our overnight bags onto a bed, claiming it for our own for the night. Ghost then shows us to the guest bathroom downstairs, which is shared with Joanie.

While Annie and Joanie finish preparing dinner and setting the table, me and the guys each take a turn at the guest shower to freshen up. We all know we smell funky after two days of being trapped in a vehicle sweating our balls off even though the air conditioning works. Yeah, we showered yesterday at the hotel, but the water in the hotel smelled of rotten eggs, so another shower is in order today.

Annie serves up a delicious salad with several options of sides, kind of like at a buffet. A homemade spaghetti and garlic bread and, of course, to top off the meal, she serves us bottled beer. It might not be my favorite beer, but I'll never turn down a good bottle of suds.

Me and the guys must have each had two servings of Annie's spaghetti and salad. It sure as hell beats the fuck out of what we've been getting at headquarters. Viper tries and so do the rest of the guys, but if it's not steak, grilled chicken, or ribs, we're shit at making a decent dinner. We tend to buy pre-made dinners for the nights we don't have the time to grill out a meal, or have more time than making a quick sandwich, or eat an MRE. The downfall of pre-made meals is the selection is slim and the repetitiveness gets old quickly.

Annie is going to be a great addition to headquarters, if me and the guys can talk her into cooking for us. She might make us fat, but hell, we'll be eating well. Annie isn't the issue though, it's her daughter. I can't seem to get my eyes off of her. The entire meal I've been catching glances at her. I know a man of my age shouldn't be interested in a woman her age. She's only eighteen, almost nineteen, and I'm thirty-one. I'm almost thirteen years her senior and I shouldn't be more than admiring her beauty, but damn, it's going to be hard for me to keep my distance from her. I'll do my best since her father is my superior's best friend and he's going to join N.R.T. so, he'll be my teammate too, soon enough.

We all call it a night shortly after dinner, after we've visited with Ghost and Annie. I try to sleep, but every time I close my eyes, his daughter haunts my dreams. This is going to be a long drive back to Texas. By two in the morning, I give up on sleep and decide to peruse things on my phone. I'm not one to do social media. I usually read or watch the news. I'm used to being up all hours of the night. The guys tease me about it because I rarely sleep. They don't know the nightmares I have. They've all served with me and been through the same hell I have. But being their medic and seeing the holes in their bodies, bringing them back to life, and seeing the life bleed out of the brothers I couldn't save, that's what usually haunts me. I had to get out of the Navy. It was the combination of the PTSD; the injuries done to my lower back, and my knees from all the jumps, were killing me.

I hear the television downstairs come on. Whoever is watching television is keeping it quiet enough to allow the rest of us to sleep. I pull on my pants and tank top and head downstairs. It's only three thirty in the morning and I figure it's Ghost up before his morning pt session or a boat drill. Instead, it's the woman I couldn't keep out of my dreams all night. She's up, flipping through the channels.

"Mind if I watch with you?" I ask as I sit on the love seat.

She shrugs her shoulders and asks, "Did I wake you with the television?"

"No, Joanie, I was already awake." I answer her.

"Couldn't sleep either."

"Nope. So, what are you watching?" I ask trying to change the subject.

"U571." She answers, even though I know the answer to the question.

I nod and turn my attention to the movie, letting the silence between us settle. Every sailor watches U571 just before they ship out after boot camp almost as a here's what life in the Navy is really like. You get shit on constantly; you do dangerous missions you can't always write home about, and sometimes you have to send your friends to their death. Why she picked this movie, I have no clue. Heck, I really know nothing about this woman other than what I was told before we came here.

We continue to watch in silence until the others in the house finally rise. Ghost is the first, along with Annie. It's like once one of them gets out of the bed, the other is instantly awake. Joanie gets up and starts a pot of coffee, knowing her parents will want a cup each before breakfast is served.

My brothers finally come downstairs with their go bags in hand. As the movie ends, I head upstairs to finish getting ready for the day ahead. I grab my tee shirt, holster, and sidearm. When I get back downstairs, Annie hands me coffee and a breakfast biscuit.

Once everyone has eaten and finished their coffee, we pack up the go bags and head out to the suburban for our trek back to Texas with our cargo. We let Annie and Joanie say goodbye to Ghost and Liam before they load up.

As Joanie comes up next to me at the door, she sticks her hands out and says, "Are you going to cuff me, officer?" Her eyes are on my sidearm.

I get her implication she feels like her parents are sending her to jail, and with us and our sidearms, we're her prison guards. I give her a smile and hand her the small bag she had packed with miscellaneous things to do while we are driving.

"No. I think we can trust you right now. If you make us lose that trust, we'll have to cuff you." I go for a bit of humor. Instead, she rolls her eyes and takes the offered bag from my hands and marches out towards the suburban.

I can't help but watch her walking away. Her hips sway just right to make me see the woman in her, not the bratty kid facade she puts on. She climbs into the farthest back seat and claims it all for herself.

Great. Now I'm going to be cramped on the middle bench seat with either Annie or Hawk. Not what my back needs or wants. It wants a comfortable bed. It needs me to stretch out.

Hawk offers the front passenger seat to Annie, who accepts. So he and I are going to be seat buddies for the next several hours until Joanie curls up and naps. That's what most people do on these long journeys, right?

Yeah, Joanie isn't normal. She puts in her headphones and listens to music while playing games on her tablet or handheld gaming system. That's what occupies her time the entire day. Although she constantly switches games. I wind up being Hawk's seat buddy the whole time we are driving for the day. We call it a night around eight when I can't deal with the pain and the guys have noticed my constant shifting.

Chapter 4: Joanie

I've spent a whole day on the road with my mom, and the men dad's new boss sent. I was figuring they were going to be men my dad's age. Nothing prepared me for the three handsome ass men that showed up yesterday afternoon.

Hell, the one that's driving me crazy is the one that still wears his hair in a semi military haircut, except the top is done with enough hair gel, making the hair into a mohawk. He's got an earring in his left ear, and those piercing hazel eyes. Every time he looks at me, it feels like he's staring into my soul. Then this morning he came down in his tank top and I got an eyeful of his pecks straining the material. Hell, one of his pecks could fill the palm of my hand.

I had to do something this morning, or else he would have known I was drooling over him. So, I put on my best bratty attitude. That got me nowhere, he didn't buy it. He teased with me and then I could see the disappointment when I took the largest seat in the vehicle for myself.

We had dinner at a buffet next door to the hotel the men have secured for us. When we walk into the hotel room, it's nice, not the typical hotel room with two queen-sized beds and a bathroom. No, this has a king-sized bed and a queen-sized bed in the sleeping area, a bathroom next to the breakfast nook, and the breakfast nook also turns into a bed itself. It's spacious.

"Annie. You and Joanie take the king." I hear his sexy baritone voice say.

The one they call Zeke tosses his go bag on the queen size bed, and Mr. sexy himself goes to making himself at home on the convertible bed of the breakfast nook.

"Where's your other guy going to sleep?" I ask.

"He's on watch." Mr. sexy answers.

Now I get it. I can't sneak out for a smoke or even a turn in the pool if I wanted to. I'm a hostage in this hotel room for the night.

Everyone is taking turns getting ready for the night when my mom starts in on me again. She still wants to know what provoked me to leave Jen's house, turn off my cellphone, not do my schoolwork and wander around San Diego.

"I needed some space, mom. What part of that can't you understand?"

"What I don't get is how Jen didn't know where you were at. Did the two of you have a disagreement?"

"No, mom. That's not it."

"Then what is it? Talk to me Joanie."

That's it. I feel my heart racing. I want to scream. But I also know it won't solve anything. I just need to get some space from my mom. I start walking towards the door when Hawk stops me short and says, "Where do you think you're going?"

I pivot and head for the only other door in the room aside from the tiny ass storage closet for luggage, the bathroom. I can hear both the men and my mom telling me the bathroom is occupied. I don't care at the moment I need my space.

I open the door and the shower is running. I head over to the toilet and plop down. Just wanting the space to breathe.

"Uh. Who's in here?" Comes his sexy voice.

"It's me the fuck up child."

"You realized I was in here taking a shower, right?"

"Yeah, I just needed some space from my mom. She's pressuring me to talk again, and I don't want to."

I can see he's got his palms pressed on the back of the shower and it's hot as fuck in here letting me know he's using the hot water.

"Wanna talk to me?" He asks concern in his voice.

"Not really. She wants to know where I was the other day, but the other day she didn't want to know."

"I get that." He says as he pokes his head out of the shower for a moment.

Damn he's sexy with that water dripping off his hair, onto his shoulders.

"What do you want to do with your life?" He asks.

"I don't know. I thought I knew, but that blew up in my face." I say, trying not to talk to him about what happened the day I got myself into this shit.

"Why don't you want to follow in your father's footsteps? You know, join the military."

"I do. The Navy won't allow me to join his little boy's club."

"Huh?"

"The Navy they won't let me be a SEAL."

"Well, you could do like all the other kids out there today who are doing things to get their way."

"What?"

"Claim your transgendered. Cut off those glorious breasts and take hormone therapy, making you 'equal.'"

"Uh. That's disgusting and it chemically castrates you, meaning I'd never have kids, and I eventually want to be a mother."

"Well, I guess you'll just have to accept you'll never be a SEAL. Anyway, it's not always what it's cracked up to be. It's hell on the back and knees, not to mention the shit we see shouldn't be seen or done by anyone."

He's somehow thrown me off guard and I say, "I was at MEPS. Jen and I skipped school to enlist in the Navy." I don't know why I'm spilling my guts to him.

"Let me guess, they turned you down because of your ADHD and ODD?" He asks.

"Yeah, and it just hurts too much to talk about it." I confess.

I didn't hear the water turn off, but suddenly the curtain jerks open and there he is, standing naked. He grabs a towel and wraps it around his waist before he grabs another towel to dry off with. Just seeing him naked for those few seconds, I can feel the heat pooling between my thighs. This man shouldn't have this kind of effect on me.

I can't take my eyes off of him as he dries himself off. He keeps the towel wrapped around his waist even as he dries his upper thighs, but I got enough of a view when he opened the shower curtain. I don't need him to take the towel off. I've got an image of his dick burned into my mind. He finally grabs his boxers off the back of the toilet and damn if he doesn't stick his towel covered cock in my face.

I think he's flirting with me. Maybe trying to help me relax with all the pressure of the move to Texas and the fact that he and two other guys are here to keep me in line. He's the first guy in a long time that sees me as a person and not the fuck up that my uncles and parents do.

When we step out of the bathroom, my mom is shooting Mr. sexy, Ace, as he's called a look saying she'll kill him if he touched me. His teammates are also shooting him a look of wonder. Asking him silently what happened. But he only says, "Why don't we all call it a night?"

I'm thankful he didn't tell anyone what I said to him in the bathroom. It would have caused an argument between my mom and me, and I couldn't deal with the drama right now. I head over to the bed my mom and I are sharing for the night and climb in not wanting to talk anymore tonight. Everyone else seems to follow in suit and hits the hay too. Mom doesn't ask me any more questions, she just slips into the bed and lays down.

It's dark out when I open my eyes up. What woke me up at this ungodly hour? My bladder. I didn't do my normal routine before heading to bed and now I'm regretting it. My bladder feels like it's going to explode. I'm in a hotel room with three men I don't really know and my mom. I can't fight my bladder if I roll over and try to sleep on my stomach like I enjoy; I'll pee in the bed. I can't get comfortable on my back or my sides. So I decide to slip out of bed and go to the bathroom.

I quietly slide out of the bed and try to make my way to the bathroom without waking anyone. The room is pitch black and since I'm sleeping on the side of the bed, that is between the two beds in the bedroom area. I shuffle my feet until I come into the more open area of the hotel room. If I head to the left, I'll go to the area where the guy on watch is sitting in a chair, sleeping. He's blocking the door, making sure I don't slip out. I turn to the right, where the breakfast nook is.

As I try quietly to close the bathroom door, it, of course, has to make a loud sound that echoes through the bathroom and I cringe, knowing I've probably disturbed someone's sleep. I flush the toilet and, of course, it's loud enough to wake the sleeping dead. I wait until the toilet stops making noise before I open the door and head back to my bed.

Only when I'm exiting the bathroom, I am having a hard time readjusting to the darkness of the room. So, while I'm standing in the breakfast nook waiting for my eyes to adjust, I hear Ace whimpering in his sleep. I look over to where he's at and he's rocking back and forth, sitting up in his bed.

"Are you okay?" I ask him.

He just rocks back and forth, and I realize he's still asleep. I crawl onto the bed and wrap my arms around him. Ignoring the zing that goes through me as our bodies touch. His eyes fly open and he looks at me, confused.

"Shh. You were having a nightmare." I whisper to him. He nods, acknowledging what I've said.

As I go to crawl back out of the bed, I feel his hand gently wrap around my wrist. "Stay, please." His voice is raspy.

I know I shouldn't because of how it will look to my mom and the other guys. But I can hear the desperation in his voice. I hate sleeping alone, it's why I rarely go back to sleep once I've woken up at night. I slide under the covers and so does he. As I reach for a pillow, I feel his muscular arm pull me closer to him. He rests my head on one of his enormous pecks and wraps his arm around me.

I can't help it, but I feel protected with his arm wrapped around me in this way. I doze off, listening to the beat of his heart in my ear. He holds me the rest of the night and for once; I sleep calmly, more at ease.

When we wake in the morning, my mom is looking at Ace with daggers. While, the other two men are making a pot of coffee and keeping thier distance from her. She is pissed and I know it. I've done it again. Crawling in bed with him is just another of my fuck ups in her eyes. Even if I explained it a million times, we didn't have sex and that it wasn't anything. In her eyes, it crossed the line.

Chapter 5: Ace

When I woke up this morning, Annie was staring at me like she wanted to kill me. Then the woman nestled into my side started waking. That's when I realized what I thought was a dream had actually happened. I had been in the middle of a nightmare and Joanie coaxed me out of it. I had asked her to stay with me. She could have said no, but I needed her.

All we did was to hold each other for the rest of the night so we could sleep. Nothing naughtily interesting happened, but by the look on Annie's face I can tell her mind has figured her daughter and I were having sex last night after everyone else was asleep. She's pissed at me, Joanie, and Hawk, who was supposed to be on watch.

"Since when did you sleep on watch? What if Joanie had snuck out the hotel door?" She's drilling Hawk.

"It's why I was posted in front of the door. No one could get by me without me feeling them." Hawk defends himself. "Plus, since this isn't a case of high security alert, we can doze off."

Annie huffs at his responses and says, "Every mission is one of high security alert."

Then she spins around to where Joanie and I are at and says, "I have no words to express how upset I am with the two of you. Which is saying a lot, considering I'm an author for a living and words usually just flow."

I adjust my morning wood before standing up and trying to defend myself and Joanie.

"Ma'am, it's not what it looks like." I start but Annie interrupts me.

"Says every man that ever got caught by the parents of a woman he wasn't supposed to be in bed with." She says.

"I promise that I never laid a hand on you daughter with ill intentions." I say.

21

"Then how the hell do you explain her cuddled up in your bed with your arm wrapped around her?"

It's not that I can't explain it, I just don't want to explain it. I know how the guys would view me if they knew I often wake up to nightmares that I can't get out of my head. How can I explain to them that just holding Joanie in my arms for a few hours kept the nightmares at bay? They would see me as less of a man, I'm sure of it.

Once everyone is dressed and ready, we leave from the hotel. I offer to drive and get a confused look from both Zeke and Hawk. I need to put some space between myself and Joanie to show Annie I'm not trying to make moves on her daughter. Plus, it'll give Annie and me a chance to talk when the guys doze off.

I pull in to the drive thru of a fast-food restaurant and order everyone breakfast biscuits, coffee and hash browns before we set off on the highway. Annie is nice enough to add the cream and sugar to my coffee and open the wrapper on my breakfast biscuit. Then she passes the bag with the food back to Hawk, who distributes biscuits and hash browns to everyone.

I drive while munching on my biscuit and hash brown, and quiet takes over the suburban. I look up into the rearview mirror and I see Joanie has her headphones on and is absorbed in one of her tablets. Zeke and Hawk are both absorbed in something on their phones.

Annie breaks the silence by asking me, "How old are you?"

I try not to get offended by her question; she is the mother of the girl who I was caught in the same bed with. "Thirty-one." I say, as I turn on the cruise control and sit back, allowing the suburban to do most of the work.

"Thirteen years." She states.

I nod, knowing she's stating our age difference. I decide on a different approach. I've already noticed with our visit, she and Ghost have a bit of an age difference. But I know pointing it out wouldn't be a smart move.

"So, how did you and Ghost meet?"

She chuckles and says, "Well, he tried to get to know me by inviting me to a party he and the guys were having. We were neighbors. However, we technically didn't meet 'romantically' until I was under his team's protection, and then it was a whirlwind relationship."

I smile, hearing her briefly explain their relationship. Then I ask my next question, "Does Ghost have nightmares?"

I can see her contemplating her answer and wondering why I've asked. "Yes, it's a downside to his job." She finally answers me.

"What do you do when he has one?"

"I typically hold him or rub the back of his head, it seems to reset him." She still has that curious look on her face.

"Has Joanie ever seen him having a nightmare?" I ask trying to figure out how she knew what to do.

"No, I don't think so. Why are you asking me these questions about my husband?" Annie shifts in her seat so she's looking straight at me.

"You see, I don't know why Joanie was up, but she found me in the middle of a nightmare. She gently woke me up and let me know. I asked her to stay with me. It's not Joanie's fault, it's mine." I tell her, taking all the blame for the situation.

"The problem isn't whose fault it is. The problem is Joanie is reckless. She will see you inviting her into your bed once as an open invitation. Even if the one time was a harmless gesture, one of the next times it will escalate and before you know it, you will be having sex with her."

I see what she's getting at and I want to scream at her I wouldn't let that happen, instead I push the accelerator pedal down and drive manually. I toss around the thought of what Annie said. I want to think I have more control over my urges, but Joanie is a beautiful woman and it could mean trouble for me if I let my guard down.

As I drive, I think to myself about all the scenarios of how I would handle it if Joanie found her way into my bed. All the what if's just like if I was preparing for a mission. Would I tell her to get out? Would I allow her to continue to sleep in my bed and set down the rules that she and I could only sleep together with no sex at all?

The bad thing is, I can't decide on what I would do. Because she felt so good in my arms last night. I really just wanted to keep holding her and sleeping. Just those few hours with her in my arms were heaven and I could have slept all day. She felt that good.

I was so lost in thought I forgot to stop for lunch and we arrived at the headquarters early and starving. I hadn't noticed the time and since I wasn't doing anything to exert energy; I wasn't hungry. At least, not until I pulled into the headquarters parking area. Then my stomach growled, telling me about skipping lunch.

When we walked into headquarters, Cynthia was making dinner, Zeke was pissed that I'd passed on lunch and Joanie, she was upset we were here at her prison for the foreseeable future. I decided to unload the suburban of everyone's luggage since Joanie and Annie were in the common room and Zeke had gone into the kitchen to help speed along dinner.

I check in with Viper and find out where he wants Annie and Joanie to stay. When we left, the plan was to let Annie and Joanie bunk together, unless Annie trusted Joanie enough for her own room. Viper tells me which rooms are for who. And damn it, he put Joanie next to me and Annie on the other side of her. I'm fucked.

There's no way I'm telling Viper it's a bad idea to put Joanie next door to me. If I tell him what happened in the hotel, he'll throttle me before Ghost gets the chance to. There's no way in hell I'm telling Ghost or Viper what happened in the hotel. Hell, they'll probably blame me for Joanie walking in on me in the shower and then me getting out and drying off in front of her as being the reason she climbed in my bed and snuggled up with me.

The truth is, there was electricity in the bathroom when she spoke to me. I couldn't help but want to wrap my arms around her and hold her. Nobody should feel as if they constantly fuck up, especially by their parents. So, giving her a view of my naked, wet body was so I could assess her. The medic in me was taking over. I wanted to make sure Joanie wasn't about to take her own life.

What I saw was pain in her eyes. Then she saw me, the man. I couldn't help it, I felt a little rise out of the way she looked at me. She didn't know in that moment how fucked up I am. My back is fucked up, my knees are jacked up and my brain, well, it won't let me sleep.

Begrudgingly I take the bags to the rooms Viper told me to. As I'm walking through the common room of headquarters, I feel someone watching me. When I look, it's Joanie, she's trying to ignore what her mom is saying and doing. Annie is talking to Cynthia and suddenly Joanie's head snaps to whatever Annie just said. By the look on Joanie's face, I can tell Annie just revealed a bit of information that Joanie didn't know. It makes me wonder what it was.

Chapter 6: Joanie

Gosh, I figured this place would have nine foot tall fences and barbed wire all around the property. However, they have a fence, it's a normal-ish privacy fence just about six feet tall. I noticed some security cameras as we came into the property. You can't take the need for security away from a SEAL.

Inside the headquarters is huge, and very welcoming. The few windows I see are huge and let in lots of light. Mom and I find our way over to what the guys call the common area and even though I'm not happy about the whole situation, the building is nice.

Almost instantly, a woman comes over to talk with my mom. Her name is Cynthia, she's Viper's lady. She seems sweet, older than me, but sweet enough. She and mom hit it off instantly. As I sit here listening to them talk and taking in the way the building is made to resemble a ship and its housing units, I also watch Ace.

I can't get the way he looked naked in the shower out of my head. The whole ride from the hotel here I kept glancing at him, but since he was driving and I was sitting in the far back of the suburban, I could only catch a side glance of him every now and then. He was one sexy specimen of a man. Even if I only got a moment to graze my eyes over his whole body before he wrapped that towel around his waist. And now I can't seem to get the image of him wet from the shower and naked out of my mind. I've seen boy's cocks in my time, but his was larger. He wasn't even hard and it was larger than what the few guys I've been with had I'm sure my eyes about popped out of my head when I saw it. Then, the way he smelled when we cuddled up in the middle of the night seems like it's forever stuck in my nostrils.

When I'd woken up this morning, I'd burrowed into his side. I didn't care that I was in his armpit. It was his scent, and it was calming to me. Mom was shooting us a look like we'd done something wrong. I'm lost in my daydreams when I see Ace walking through the common room carrying my luggage. He looks over at me and our eyes meet.

Fuck, how am I supposed to live under the same roof with this man if he makes me get wet just looking at me? I squirm and I see him shake his head. Yeah, I think he knows what he does to me. I know I shouldn't be crushing on one of my dad's future teammates because, well, he's going to be one of my dad's teammates and he's older than me. How much older I don't know. Old enough to have at least served for four years in the military. But knowing the military and these men, he did more than that so he wouldn't be involved in the inactive ready reserves. So, he's got to be at least eight years older than me. I'm guessing he's at least twenty six-ish. I'll have to ask him later.

And just like that, I'm pulled from my musings by something my mom says. She's told this Cynthia woman that her time in captivity almost made her lose me. I knew mom and dad met on a mission, and she was kidnapped while under protective custody, but I never knew that mom almost miscarried me. One more thing they've kept from me. I guess they blame the near miscarry as the reason I came out as fucked up as I am.

Next I hear my mom and Cynthia talking about having sex. Ew. Now I've got the image of my dad and mom naked, having sex in my head.

"Mom Ew. Do you have to go into those kinds of details? I could have gone a lifetime without picturing you and dad naked doing the deed." I say.

Mom and Cynthia both just laugh at what I said. Yes, I probably overreacted, but I do read smutty romance books and I have had sex. Much to my dad's chagrin, I lost my virginity a few years ago. But he probably thinks I've given it to every guy since then. In truth, I've only had sex three times. The time I lost my virginity to piss my dad off. Then at the prom, my junior year with my prom date. And with a guy who I thought I was in love with over the summer, but he wound up being a one-night stand.

None of those times felt right. I decided after my one-night stand over the summer to wait until I found the right guy to give my heart to. It's weird, a person like me known to do impulsive things waiting on sex.

Dinner is called and since I hardly know any of the men here, I was hoping Ace would sit near me, so I'd have someone to talk to during dinner. Except he chose to sit as far away from me as he could. It hurt. Occasionally during the dinner I catch his eyes looking at me. I wonder what he's thinking.

After dinner, Viper shows us up to our rooms. Thankfully, my mom and dad trusted me enough to give me a room of my own. The room is a nice size with a king sized bed in it and a small area for me to have some foods in my room so I don't always have to go down to the kitchen for a snack. I doubt I'll use that since I have absolutely zero dollars to my name. My bathroom and my mom's bathroom share a joining wall. Whenever she's in the shower, I can hear the water hitting the walls.

I can hear mom and Viper talking in her room. He wants to know what happened on the way here. Everyone is being mum about the whole situation. I feel bad because he has to report back to my dad that we made it here safely. Viper can tell something happened since everyone is tense around me. I want to tell Viper what happened and take the blame for crawling in Ace's bed, but I don't want to get Ace in trouble. So I keep the information to myself since everyone else seems to be protecting Ace by keeping mum.

I lay down on my bed, and eventually I'll try to get some sleep. Unpacking can wait until tomorrow. It's not like I brought a lot with me. I grab my e-reader and start reading one of my smutty ebooks. You know the kind where the woman meets the man of their dreams and falls head over heels. It's crazy how life isn't like the way a romance novel is written. I've fallen a couple of times for a couple of boys, but it was never like the books describe it. The few times I had sex, I never felt the tingles the books described, it wasn't mind bending sex. It hurt deep inside. It hurt every time the boy pushed inside me. It hurt.

The first time I'd passed it off as the pain associated with losing my virginity, but it never got replaced with the orgasmic joy the romance novels described. So, I decided prom night would be better. It wasn't. I still hurt the entire time. I cried and the dumb fuck thought I was crying because of the pleasure he was giving me. Then I tried again and again, it was a repeat of prom night. I figure I'm not meant to have sex, maybe not yet, because I've not been with the right man.

I've dozed off reading the novel, it's my normal. Read until my eyes won't stay open. Tonight when I doze off, I drop the e-reader onto my face, popping myself in the face. My eyes fly open and now I'm awake again. Ugh. What I wouldn't give for social media right now. I would typically scroll through until I drifted off again. I hate this punishment. All I can do is lie here and stare at the ceiling.

After tossing and turning for who knows how long, I finally fall asleep. I wake up as per my normal in the middle of the night. I hear someone shouting in the room that my headboard shares a wall with. Curiosity wins out and I slide out of bed, knowing I won't be able to go back to sleep anyway.

I head out of my door and into the balcony that overlooks the common area. All the lights down there are on dim. I guess the guys leave them on in case someone gets up to get a midnight snack. I walk over to the next door, not my mom's door, but the other direction where the person screaming was coming from. Trying the doorknob, it's not locked.

All the crazy scenarios are running through my mind. It could be one of the men went to town and picked up a woman and, well, they're having rough sex. I know it's not a good idea to just walk into someone's room, but I'm not about to let the person who sounded like they were in pain suffer.

I open the door and who do I see sitting up in the bed rocking? It's Ace, and apparently when he's here he sleeps in the buff. I quietly close the door and head over to his bed. Sitting down next to him, I gently rub his back and try to comfort him while he continues to rock back and forth. I've seen my mom do this with my dad several times growing up. They don't know I've seen it, but as a child, I was a mischievous one and would get out of bed and roam the house. I've seen her coax dad out of several nightmares over the years. I don't want to wake him too suddenly. I quietly say his name and he finally comes out of his trance of a dream.

He looks over at me and says, "How did you get in here?"

I chuckle a little at his question, as he's still a bit out of it. "I was awake and you were having a nightmare. I heard it through the wall, so I tried the door and you didn't lock it." I explain.

"Oh. I'm sorry to have disturbed your sleep." He stands up and walks into his bathroom for a moment and lord, I can't help but watch his sexy naked ass walk away.

When he comes back out, he's wearing a pair of boxers and I can't help but be saddened a bit that he felt the need to cover himself up. He's washed his face and neck of the sweat. He plops back down onto the bed and lays his head down on his interlaced fingers.

"Why did you come to the sound? Why didn't you just knock on the door?" He ponders.

I shrug my shoulders. "It sounded like you needed help. I couldn't let you be in need and just knock." I explain.

"Have you ever thought about doing something in the medical field?"

"With my problems, they probably wouldn't have me."

He sits up and gently grabs my chin between his thumb and forefinger, tilting my head down to look in his eyes. "Hey, you weren't about to let your problems be the reason not to get into the military. Why change that now?"

He's right, I just feel defeated right now. Ever since that day at MEPS, I have just felt so defeated. He looks at the clock on his phone and rolls his eyes. It's three in the morning.

"C'mon, let's try to get some sleep." He lifts his sheets and allows me to slide in between the sheets. They're not you're plain jane white cotton sheets. From what I can tell in the dark, they're a dark color, probably black, and they feel like satin or silk against my skin. It makes the room seem a bit cooler under just a sheet and a light blanket.

Once I'm settled, I feel him pull me closer and before long; we are both sleeping. When we wake up, it's late in the morning and I hear people passing by the door talking.

Ace pops up out of bed and quickly pulls on a shirt and pants before he sits back on the bed where I'm still trying to wake up. He looks at his phone and curses under his breath. "I'm late."

He looks at me and takes a deep breath. "I thought I'd have more time to think about this moment. Joanie, I don't know what it is about you, but..." He trails off.

"I know. We can't be seen together. Someone might get the wrong idea about what is happening behind closed doors." I say, hanging my head.

"No, that's not what I was going to say." Ace's voice raises a little. "With you I can sleep. I haven't been able to sleep in years. I'm haunted with nightmares."

"Oh, but what if someone sees me leaving your room? Aren't you worried about the fallout it may cause?"

"I am. But, the sleep I get just holding you in my arms may be worth a good knock down drag out fight with my brothers."

I've never known a boy willing to fight with his friends over me. It warms me inside, knowing that he's willing to fight with them to get the sleep we both need. He takes my hands in his and kisses my knuckles, and I swear for the first time, I feel the zing the romance novels talk about.

Ace walks with me to the door and makes sure my mom isn't anywhere around to scold me about where I spent my night. I quickly scoot into my room and flop down on my bed. I think I'm in love, and he doesn't even know it. I know it's so wrong, but it feels so right.

I start the day doing my schoolwork and communicating in school chat with my friends. Thankfully, I can still send them e-mails through the school e-mail, but school monitors that, so we can only talk about school projects or in code. By shortly after lunch I'm done with all my assignments so, I turn to unpacking and putting away the clothes I brought with me. I've got less than six months of school left and I have to think about what I'm going to do after I'm done with high school.

As I'm putting away my things, I think about what Ace asked me about earlier. Military men have surrounded me my whole life and running towards a problem has always seemed to come naturally. So, what would I do in the medical field that isn't in the military that still runs towards problems?

I think about it and grab my computer. I begin researching colleges near me. All of them have a medical program. I notice that all of them offer an EMT/Paramedic program. I wonder if that is what Ace was hinting at.

The next few days seem drag on because every time I try to talk to Ace, he's busy in a meeting or hanging out with one of the other guys. I just want to pick his brain since he's the only person who sees the potential in me. Every night I wake up in the middle of the night and wander over to his room and crawl under the covers. I've timed it the last few nights before the nightmare took hold.

When we wake up in the mornings, he helps me sneak back into my room before anyone sees I'm leaving from his room. I have to admit it is the best sleep I've ever gotten. I even might quit my melatonin if he and I sleep the whole night together. *Yeah, right, that'll never happen.*

Chapter 7: Ace

I've woken up every morning since Joanie arrived with her in my bed. She wears a tank top without a bra and a pair of shorty shorts. I've had to wear boxers to bed, so if someone else walks in they won't get the wrong impression. Although I'd love to sleep skin to skin with her. It's been the best feeling I've ever had, except for the even stiffer morning wood I've had. After escorting Joanie out of my room, I head to the shower and have to jerk myself off because otherwise my ramrod won't go down quick enough. I wonder if I would sleep the entire night if I went to sleep with her at night. But she's a high school kid and I'm an adult. She hits the sack at ten and I stay awake until the exhaustion kicks my ass.

I've seen her following me around, but for the sake of appearances, I can't have anyone see us together. Especially not Annie. Hawk and Zeke already suspect something, since I've been late to work a few mornings this week. Her mom would kill me after the look she gave me in the hotel room. I'm trying to protect Joanie, but she doesn't seem to understand why I'm keeping her at arm's length.

Annie didn't seem to be turned off by our age difference, only by Joanie's impulsiveness. If there was a way for me to show Annie that Joanie and I have true feelings for each other, maybe it would help my case with Ghost. Maybe it would keep him from killing me.

Today we began to clear the land for the houses Ghost's team will live in. We know at least four of his team will come to Texas and join N.R.T. soon. It's a heavily wooded area, so we're using an excavator with a tool for cutting trees down. From there, we load the trees onto logging trucks and hauled to a nearby lumber mill where we'll get a little moolah for our work. Since we're using containers for the main house, we don't need the raw trees, but we will need plenty of two by fours and plyboard, so the lumber yard is also giving us a discount off of the lumber we order.

It's a hot April day and apparently Joanie has spring break and nothing better to do today. She's walked out in a skimpy pair of cut-off jean shorts and an almost white see-thru tank top with flip-flops on. To top things off, I notice a few of my brothers drooling over her, the ones that don't know she's Ghost's daughter, and he'd kill them. She's carrying a pitcher and some glasses on a tray.

I drop what I'm doing and head over to where she's at and say, "Joanie, don't you think you should have covered yourself up better before coming out here?"

"What? I'm dressed casually." She tries to argue back.

I can see her nipples through the shirt, but I try to avert my eyes. Although just the quick sight has my cock stirring to life. As the other men come up, she offers to them a glass of lemonade. I even take one for myself and can't help but allow myself a perusal of her body as she pours drinks for the other men.

"Why'd you come out here?"

"I figured you guys were thirsty."

"Yeah, but some of them are looking at you like you're a piece of meat." I can't help it, but the words come out in a growl.

I notice Viper approaching, and I drop the conversation as she offers him a glass of lemonade. He's watching me intently. He's pissed off about the fact my eyes are on Joanie. I can't help it. I'm attracted to her like a moth to a flame.

"Why don't you cut some trees? I'll take over down here." Viper suggests.

From the tone of his voice, I knew it wasn't a suggestion; it was an order to get me away from Joanie. I head towards the excavator and feel his and Joanie's eyes on me as I walk away.

The excavator is exhausting, repetitive work. It keeps Joanie from following me and allows me time to think to myself. What I want to do about this thing growing between us?

I've always heard when you find the one, your soulmate, everything is right. With Joanie, I can sleep for the first time in many years. She seems to keep the nightmares away. If I want to see if I can try to sleep a whole night, I can't do it here under Viper's watch. Joanie and I would have to go to a hotel and stay the night. Viper shows his disdain for me showing Joanie any attention.

I'm not sure if his disdain is because he's only heard her parent's side of the story, or if it's because he's still trying to figure things out with his own woman.

Cynthia, we found her on our last mission. The government had determined she had died after going missing in Egypt over thirteen years ago. The government declared her dead after she'd been missing for ten years. That's when he got out of the Navy and start N.R.T. he was dead set that she was still alive.

Three years later, we went on a mission on the Mexico, New Mexico border and found a woman chained up like a dog. That was how we found Cynthia, looking starved to death and being treated like no living thing should be treated. At first Viper couldn't believe it was her, and now he's fighting with the government to keep her from going to the brig for going AWOL during her time in the service.

Viper had crawled into a bottle when she went missing, me and the other guys didn't know at the time that she was the reason. It's only recently come to light and Viper has stopped drinking as much. He's got a new lease on life having his woman here with us. We've just got to get her issues worked through and help her back into a normal life.

My thoughts drift back to Joanie. What's she going to do after high school? I've dropped a hint she might look into the medical field, and from what Zeke has seen on her web searches, she's exploring colleges in the area and their medical programs. She's spent quite a bit of time exploring the EMT/paramedic programs. It seems to fit her with her wanting to help people and running into my room when I'm having a nightmare.

The whole week goes by in a drone of trees being felled. The only light in the day is when Joanie shows up with sandwiches for me and the guys. She tells me it's her idea. Since she's on spring break and has nothing better to do than sit around and watch tv or read books. The men and I are thankful since she introduces us to a new type of sandwich, "the Dutch special" as she calls it. She butters the bread instead of using mayonnaise and then she adds just meat and cheese, no tomato or lettuce. The cheese isn't the oil-based American cheese, it's the pre-sliced deli cheeses of all kinds. They're delicious, and thankfully she's not trying to force a bunch of meat loving men to eat vegetables.

We casually talk during my lunch breaks and I find out she really is interested in the medical field. Joanie wants to help people, but she doesn't know if she gets into being a paramedic and then decides it's not for her how her parents will feel about her changing her mind. She really doesn't want to disappoint her parents anymore. They don't realize her whole senior year in high school until her trip to MEPS has been to prove to her parents that she is trying to control her problems and straighten out her life. Her parents have lived with her issues for so long they expect the other shoe to fall when she messes up, or they expect her to make the mistakes that will get her in the biggest trouble. It's hard for them to see that she's learned to think about her decisions before just jumping in.

My heart aches for her. She's been trying to show her family she's trying. But every time she seems to screw it up some way, somehow. Ever since she arrived here she's been following the rules Viper and her mom have set in place, and I think Annie and Viper see she's trying.

The more we talk, the more I want to kiss her lips and feel her melting into me. But I know we can't and I have to keep telling myself that. It's why I don't ask her to come to my room at night before I head to bed.

Chapter 8: Joanie

My decision to make the men working on the housing site lunches every day during my spring break has been well accepted by almost everyone. Viper doesn't seem to like me hanging around *his* men and the worksite. He watches me like a hawk, as if he doesn't trust me. Then there's Ace, who constantly tells me the other men are looking over me like I'm a piece of meat and my choice of clothing is inappropriate for the worksite. When I'm there, he hangs out near me making small talk, but I think it's to keep the other men from eye fucking me. It's nice, sort of, but overprotective, in a way, just like my dad and uncles.

Making them lunch and taking it to the worksite gives me some time to keep from being bored out of my mind and gives me a sense of purpose. Even if it is for just a couple of hours each day.

The day the containers arrive, Viper and Ace won't let me near the site. They both site my safety as their main concern. I'm still allowed to make lunch for the men, but I can't leave the back patio to keep out of their way. I do as they say, setting up the picnic tables with pitchers of tea, lemonade, and my speciality sandwiches.

At lunch I ask Viper if I can start helping around my parents' house since I usually finish my school work around lunchtime and I have nothing else to do. He's somewhat agreeable with my offer of help. He sets down the law that he's the boss and what he tells me to do; I have to do just like a regular job. I agree with his terms. As he goes to leave, he says, "Wear pants, a tee shirt and a pair of boots. The last thing I need is for you or one of the men getting hurt."

"I don't have any boots." I inform Viper.

"Fine. Wear your tennis shoes. But please leave those see through shirts and nearly not there shorts behind and put on something decent to work in."

When I packed, I was angry, so I grabbed all of my shorty shorts, but I also grabbed some of my jeans. Making a mental note that Viper wants me to wear more decent clothing around the men, I make a silent vow to obey him and stay on his good side. Ace has been lecturing me about the men staring at me, so I understood what Viper meant by the men getting hurt.

I've been wearing tee shirts, jeans and tennis shoes for weeks while working on the house that will soon be my parents. When one evening before we leave Viper hands me a box. It's got the word Bates on it. I know this brand, it's the brand the military uses. I open it up and lo-and-behold there are a pair of calf high steel toe boots. The kind I've always dreamed of: they're black leather over the toe and heel with a rubberized sole that's oil and slip resistant. The sides are a mesh breathable material that's also black. I wonder how Viper knew these were my favorite.

I give Viper a hug and head up to my room to try them on. They fit my foot perfectly. I wonder how Viper knew the right size to order? I've never bought these before, my parents wouldn't let me. I can only guess he guessed my size or Ace snuck in and got him my flip-flops for a comparison. Either way, I'm ecstatic.

I've been here about a month, and as much as I don't like the fact I can't contact my friends outside of school time, I'm finding ways to cope. I've been working on mom and dad's house for the last few weeks and with spring in the air, I've noticed some flowers in bloom. Thinking it would be nice to have a bouquet in the headquarters, making it a bit more homey and less like a place where a group of men live.

It's a Friday afternoon and Viper isn't anywhere around the worksite. So, when I finish what he's assigned me to do, I clean up my area and look for a larger patch of these beautiful blue flowers. Staying near the stream that flows on the property, I find a field that is full of flowers and I pick the more opened ones for a centerpiece of the dining room table. If I get enough, I might make a small bouquet for Viper and Cynthia's room, my room, and my mom's room. Maybe it would show them for once I'm thinking of someone other than myself.

I'm stooped down and in my own world when I hear the rumble of a motor. Then I hear someone calling my name. When I turn, it's Viper, and he doesn't look happy. He cuts the engine to the ATV he's riding and makes a quick phone call. *Oh Fuck, they're all looking for me.*

"Get on." Viper orders. "You've got your momma worried sick. No one knew where you were at." He chews me out, just like my dad would.

"What? I wasn't doing anything I wasn't supposed to be doing." I bite out as I get onto the ATV and he fires up the engine.

"Not this time." He bites back and grabs my hands, making me drop the flowers I was holding. He places my hands around his waist to hold on to.

"I've been good this whole time, Viper. I haven't wandered off the property. This afternoon I finished up early and saw some flowers I wanted to pick for headquarters. I was still on the property and behaving, that should mean something." I holler into Viper's ear.

He's ignoring my argument as he concentrates on the trail ahead. I'm fuming by the time we pull into the parking garage at headquarters. I can't help but as we drove back to the headquarters, Viper's shirt flies up as he drives from the speed he's going and my hands are against his skin. I've gotten a feel of his washboard abs. Gosh, if these men aren't all fit. I know how it feels to hold Ace, and any woman is lucky to have one of these men hold them.

When we get off the ATV, Viper takes me by the shoulder and pulls me close to him. He says, "After the panic I saw on your momma's face, I don't want to see that again. And as long as your dad isn't here, I'm stepping in his place. So what I say goes. If you're going to wander off, you better tell someone where you are going. Do you understand me?"

It's clear as day. I've fucked up in his eyes. Even though I was on the property where I was supposed to be. I nod at what he's said. There's no use in arguing.

A few minutes later my mom comes down with a tear streak faced. She was worried I'd run away. I know I can't understand how she feels. I'm not a mother. But I've been trying to be good for her and save her the worry she's gone through over the last several years of my life.

"I'm sorry, mom." I say, taking her into a hug.

"It's okay. I'm glad you were on the property. You just need to let someone know when you're going to wander off like that." She gives me another hug and then we settle into a comfortable silence.

I get up and head to the weight room, it's a place I go to sometimes to clear my mind. Viper always sends one of the guys in to watch over me, making sure that I don't hurt myself on the equipment. I usually leave shortly afterwards because the guys staring at me, makes me feel uncomfortable, unless it's Ace.

I'm sitting on the weight bench using the free weights doing curls. When I look up, Ace is standing in the doorway. I know exactly what he's about to say.

Putting the weights down, I ask, "What?"

He comes closer and says, "You had me worried."

I wasn't expecting that. Everyone usually tells me how my screwup affects my parents and how I should have done this differently or that differently. As if I haven't already gone through those thoughts myself.

"I had you worried? I was here on the property." I scoff at him.

"Yeah, but no one knew that and Viper questioned me because he knows we're close. I couldn't tell him where you might be at and I saw the look in his eyes that he thought I was lying to him." He tells me.

Realizing he's backed me into the back wall of the weight room, I reply, "You could have told him honestly there's nothing going on between us." But my heart is racing at the closeness.

"Oh really? I don't think that would be honest." He presses into me and I can feel the hardness in his pants.

"But there's nothing going on between us." I say, but deep down I wish it wasn't true.

"We've done nothing. You're right. However, sleeping with you at night is my little slice of heaven. I smell your arousal every night and every morning I have to relieve myself in the shower. I'm not sure how much longer I can keep from having all of you." Ace leans his head down towards mine and suddenly our lips brush together.

We both moan at the light touch. He's confessed he wants me as much as I want him. But is it just seeking a momentary solace, or is it something more? I have to fight the urge just to give myself to him. The kiss is light and quick, but it's our first kiss and I can't help but want to feel this feeling forever.

Ace pulls away and says, "Joanie, there are so many things that could have happened to you out there. My mind was going crazy with all the things that could have become of you, and to think I may not have ever gotten the chance to kiss you."

He turns and leaves the weight room. I can't help but stand there, still stunned. I touch my fingers to where his lips touched mine and I smile, just remembering the way his soft, full lips felt on mine.

Chapter 9: Ace

The next few weeks have gone by and not a minute has gone by without me wanting another kiss, but I knew when I kissed her, it was wrong. However, I still want to taste her, hold her and tell everyone she's mine.

If anything, the kiss hasn't driven her away, it's drawn her closer to me. We've been talking more, and she's come into my room earlier in the evening. Nothing sexual has happened, but I know she wants it as much as I do.

I'm more worried about what her father will do to me if we have sex before I get his permission to be with her than I am with Annie. Annie seems okay with our age difference, but Ghost is going to be my teammate and I need his okay before I cross any lines.

I found out a few days ago Cynthia is pregnant with two babies and my leader and friend is going to be a father. On Friday evening, we are having a party to celebrate the news. Ghost even shows up for the event and stops in to see the progress of his new house.

The beers are flowing and I'm feeling the effects. Joanie seems a bit depressed at all the celebration for Cynthia and Viper. I wait until I see Ghost and Annie go into their room before I make like I'm escorting Joanie to her room. We pause on the balcony overlooking the common area and I ask her, "What's wrong?"

She tries to play it off, but I don't buy it. "Nothing." She answers.

I'm only a little tipsy, but I push her up against the wall and press her. "Something's bothering you, Jo. What is it?"

She bites on the inside of her cheek, like I've seen her do so many times when she's trying to debate on something.

"Jo, it's me. Come on, talk to me." I plead with her.

She finally looks up at me and says, "Is it supposed to hurt when you have sex?"

40

Oh shit. Now I know why she's been so reserved about wanting sex.

"Come into my room." I say, my medic brain is going into action. I want to know everything.

She comes into my room with me and sits on my bed. Any buzz I had a moment ago is now gone. I've got a ton of questions for her, starting with who she's been having sex with.

"Jo, did someone here force you to have sex?" I ask, concerned.

"Oh, no. I stopped having sex before I came here because every time I had sex, it hurt." She explains.

She spends the next few minutes telling me about her limited experiences with sex and what she thought the pain had been the first time, but when the pain was there again the second and third time, she knew something was wrong.

"Sex isn't supposed to hurt, Jo. If you weren't so descriptive about your previous sexual experiences, I would say they weren't turning you on. But, from your description, you were aroused so, I need to ask, where is the pain during sex?"

She shrugs. "It just hurts. I don't know how to describe it."

I think for a moment my dick wants to do a show and tell, but my brain knows better, it knows I need to have her tell me where the pain is. Finally, I come up with an idea to relax her and get her to show me where the pain is during sex.

I gently push her back onto the bed and immediately see the concern in her eyes. "Jo, I'm a medic. What I'm about to do is the same thing a doctor would do, nothing inappropriate." Although right now I want to lay her out and kiss away all her pain.

She nods for me to continue. I push her shirt up just below her bra and gently press on her abdomen. Watching her face, I don't see her flinching with pain. As I move around her belly, I watch her reactions to the same amount of pressure and feel for any abnormalities. Finishing up my examination of her abdomen, I've found nothing out of the normal, but I'm not done with my assessment.

"Does it hurt when the man penetrates you, or is it deeper inside?"

She answers this question quickly, "Deep inside. Penetration isn't a problem. It's when the guy's in it really hurts."

"Have you ever had a pelvic exam?"

"No, I went once with my mom to her gynecologist and the doctor said I was a healthy young lady. I didn't need an exam until I became sexually active or I reached a certain age."

"Ok. Here's what I suggest. I'd like to have doc come out here and see you. If I just google your symptoms, it gives me a bunch of different things it could be. Looking over them, I can eliminate all but a few and to diagnose which of them it is, you'd need a pelvic exam." I explain to Joanie why I want her to see the doctor.

"Its cancer, isn't it?" She's freaking out.

"No, Jo. But it could be something that doesn't need to be put off any longer." Without scaring her, I try to let her know how important it is for her to see a doctor ASAP.

She starts crying anyway, and all I can do is hold her. By the time she finally stops crying, it's late, and she's fallen asleep. I gently shift her up into the bed and cover us up. Before I doze off, I send Doc a message about needing him to see Joanie for a pelvic exam. I know he'll get back to me whenever he can to schedule an appointment.

I wake up to the sound of a knock on my door. Joanie is still asleep in the bed. I climb out and head over to the door, but by the time I'm about to open it, whoever is on the other side has grown impatient enough to try the knob. I've never been one to lock my bedroom door, so the door swings open.

There stands Ghost. *Oh Fuck*! His mouth hangs open as if he was about to ask me a question, but his eyes land on my bed and who is sleeping in it. He didn't have to see her face. She's the only one here with purplish hair.

"**VIIIIPPPER!!!**" He turns and heads towards the stairs and the uppermost level, where my boss is probably still sleeping.

"Wait, Ghost." I say, catching his attention.

He turns to me and glares. If looks could kill, I'd be road kill. "What." He grounds out between clenched teeth and I can see his fists are already clenched. He's ready to knock me to the other side of tomorrow.

"I-It's not what it looks like." I'm scared shitless of this man and I know the waver in my voice tells him so. I'm not usually one to back down from a fight, but Ghost has a reputation. He didn't get the call sign of Ghost without killing a few men in his day, and the rumor is he is as quiet as a ghost when he sneaks up on his kills.

"Oh, it's not?" He takes a few steps towards me, closing the distance. "I come in to ask you for some medication for Annie, only to find my **Daughter in your bed**! What am I supposed to think? Because I'll tell you what I think right now. You're fucking my daughter right here under my best friend's nose." He shakes his head and I can tell his anger is about to bust.

"Yeah, she's in my bed. Go look. She's fully dressed. Last night she asked me a medical question and we talked about what she'd asked. She fell asleep, so I covered her up and we both slept. **NOTHING** happened."

"What kind of question did she have that couldn't wait until this morning?" Ghost asks me.

"I'm sorry, but I don't think she would want me to divulge that information. I'm waiting for Doc to get back to me about when he can see her." I can see as the realization sinks in with him. This could be something she's been hiding for some time and she needs to see a doctor.

By now we've gotten some spectators. Even Annie has come out of her room and is watching the altercation between the two of us.

"How about you two men come and talk about it like reasonable adults?" Annie suggests, pointing to her room.

She's right, and both Ghost and I know it. We both hang our heads having been scolded by mother and head into her room. I sit in a chair at the small table while Annie and Ghost both sit on the end of her bed. She takes his hand and says, "Listen to me."

Ghost turns and looks at her. "Since we've been here Joanie has been getting good grades in school, and she's been working on our house. Not to mention she's not been in any trouble."

"Yeah, hun, but what has she been doing with **HIM**?" Ghost jabs his thumb in my direction.

Annie shrugs her shoulders, not knowing what to say to her own husband about mine and Joanie's relationship. "I'd have to say, if he says nothing sexual happened, then nothing happened."

Ghost growls at Annie's remark and looks at me and asks me, "Is it true?"

"Yes, it's true Ghost. I've never laid an inappropriate hand on your daughter." I pause for a moment and meet both Ghost's and Annie's eyes before I say the next bit. I know when the next words come out, Ghost could either kill me or give me permission. "I care about your daughter. She's been sneaking into my bed at night. She wards off the nightmares I have. As much as I want to pursue something with your daughter, I haven't, because I respect you. I want your permission before I pursue Jo."

Ghost stands having heard my words and I stand ready to defend myself. "You're telling me finding the two of you in the bed together isn't a first?"

"No, sir. I sleep better with her next to me in the bed." I'm being honest with him I can only hope he gives me that much. "I really do care about her."

His breathing is heavy and I'm tensing in preparation for the punch I know is coming. Fighting with Ghost isn't going to buy me brownie points with Joanie, so I prepare to take whatever he throws and not punch the man back. His fist greets my chin, but it's not what I was expecting. His knuckles graze the bottom of my chin lightly. Then he wraps his arm around me in a headlock and pulls me in close enough I can hear his threat.

"You hurt my daughter in any way and I'll hunt you down and kill you."

"Yes, sir." I say, trying my hardest to nod my head.

My heart wants to jump for joy, as I now have Ghost's permission to pursue a relationship with Joanie. It's now up to her now if she wants me.

We hear a commotion at the door and when Ghost and I look at the door, there stands a sleepy and confused Viper, Razor and Zeke. They all came running, having heard Ghost hollering for Viper and seeing the events unfolding on the balcony.

"What the fuck is going on here?" Viper asks.

Ghost still has me in the headlock, so it appears to them as we are in the middle of a fight.

"Oh, nothing. We've worked things out Viper." Ghost answers, releasing me from the headlock.

"Dude, you know how hard it is to throw this prosthesis on in a rush?" Razor asks. "No one wants my stump flailing around trying to break up a fight."

We all burst out laughing at what he's said because the imagery of it all. One can only imagine trying to break up a fight and separating arms and there's a stump in there trying to help.

As the laughing subsides, I see a confused, sleepy Joanie walking into the room. "What's going on?" She asks. The men part to let her into her parents' room. I take a few strides and grab the sides of Joanie's face. Tilting it up towards mine, I plant a claiming kiss on her lips. Most of the men whoop and cheer us on while Viper looks on in confusion.

"It's about damn time." Zeke mutters.

"What?" Viper asks.

"She's been slipping into his room every night." Zeke informs everyone. "Y'all think I've only got cameras in the parking area, nope I've got them in all the halls, and common areas, for our protection."

Viper looks at me with anger and asks, "Is that true? Ever since you picked her and Annie up?"

I give him a curt nod. I'm not proud that Joanie's been helping me with my nightmares. Being attracted to her isn't embarrassing to me, but the nightmares are.

"Is this what you guys didn't want to tell me about after the trip?"

Zeke speaks up and says, "Yeah, Joanie was in his bed the next morning. But in all honesty, we've been on missions together and for Ace to be the last one to wake up says something."

I see the recognition cross Viper's face. He was the only one I confided in that I had nightmares to keep me up all hours. Viper grins and smacks me on the back. He looks to Ghost and says, "I told you she had a motivation."

Ghost chuckles at what Viper says and nods. "Yeah, he just asked me if it was okay to date her."

As I take Joanie back into my room, I hear Viper say, "I hope he didn't get the cart before the horse."

"He better not have. He says nothing has been going on between them, and I have to trust it."

I see Joanie smile at the last bit her dad says. He trusted we haven't been doing anything we shouldn't have, and he didn't tear into her about it either.

Chapter 10: Joanie

He kissed me right there in front of my parents and several of the men of N.R.T. I thought I was going to die of embarrassment when the guys whooped and whistled at the show of affection he gave me. I was sure dad was going to come after him and kill him.

When I hear the way my dad and Viper are talking, it becomes apparent that my dad already knew about our attraction. Ace tugs on my arm and leads me into his room. I'm still in shock when he closes his room door.

"What's going on?" I ask, trying to clear the brain fog.

Usually as soon as I wake up I'm rearing to go, but these last few weeks just sleeping with Ace I'm not so quick to wake up. I'm seeing exactly why my parents need coffee in the morning. I don't need the coffee, I just need a few minutes to let my synapses start firing.

"Joanie, your father gave us permission to date. You no longer have to sneak into my room." Ace says, as the smile on his face grows wider.

Ace's phone chings with a message and he looks down at it for a moment before he types a reply. I watch as his fingers fly over the keypad. He waits a moment and then nods as if he's talking with someone else in person.

When he looks back at me, he says, "Doc will be here Monday morning to see you."

"Shit, that was fast." I say.

Ace sits next to me on the bed and places his hands on my shoulders. "We're both concerned about you. With your age, it could be several things, but each one of them could damage your reproductive organs if not treated quickly. None of them are cancer, so don't start thinking the worst."

I hear my mom's voice as she gasps, "Oh my God. What's wrong, honey?"

Ace stands up and approaches my mom. "Annie, this is something private, Joanie spoke with me in confidence about. It's up to her if she wants to talk about it now, or wait until she has some results and can give some definitive answers."

Mom nods, not pushing the subject like she normally does. "I'm sorry, I knocked, but you didn't answer. I just needed something for a bit of reflux I'm having and thought you might have something."

I've never seen my mom so apologetic like this before. Ace goes over to his medical kit and rummages around until he finds what he's looking for. He hands my mom a small bottle with a few pills in it and says, "Take one pill when the reflux hits, if it persists after an hour, take another. Don't take any more after the second one. If it continues, you need to tell me or get it checked out."

"It's nothing much, Ace. I just get this when I drink a little too much." My mom placates Ace, but I see his concern written all over his face.

Mom takes the small bottle of pills and just before she leaves, she says to me, "If you want to talk, I'm willing to listen."

I'll think about it since here over the last few years our talks are more of screaming fits. She wants to know more and I don't want to divulge more, but she pushes until I scream at her. This time she's leaving it up to me.

Ace walks her out and when he closes the door, I hear the lock click. "I think we're going to have to start locking this door." He says, as he saunters over to where I'm sitting.

He stops right in front of where I'm sitting and pulls me up. I hate feeling so small, but next to his large frame, it's nice. At MEPS, they measured me at five seven. He's shorter than my dad, so my best guess is he's got to be a good six foot two.

He tilts my chin up to his mouth and before I can say a word, his lips are on mine. They're tender, just like the day in the weight room. He places little kisses on my lips as he begins to speak.

"Jo, say you want me."

Just hearing the desire in his voice sends a flood of wetness to my core. "I want you." I reply, there is a raspiness to my voice that I've never heard before.

"Good. I didn't want to believe it was a one-way attraction." He says as he places more kisses on my lips.

His kisses become more insistent as his tongue presses at the seam of my lips and I open up instantly for him. His tongue darts in the moment I open up my mouth. My tongue tangles with his as we taste each other.

We push back and forth with our tongues in a dance of tasting and tangling. I feel Ace's hands under my shirt as he holds me close to him by my waist. I feel like I'm floating in the air as we continue to kiss so passionately it's as if we don't need air, we just need the other person.

Ace gently pushes me back and I fall onto the bed. We bounce on the mattress and he rolls me over on top of him. Breaking the kiss, I sit back and pull my shirt over my head. Instantly, Ace's hands go straight to my breasts. Gently kneading them in his large hands.

My hands slide up his washboard abs and to his large pectoral muscles. I still can't believe how large they are and how they fill my hands like my breasts fill his hands. I gently tweak one of his nipples and Ace lets out a groan as he leans forward to suck one of my nipples into his mouth.

Before we can go any further, a knock comes on the door. I groan in disbelief at how this Saturday morning is turning his room into Grand Central Station. Ace picks me up and places me beside him on the bed. "Put your shirt on." He orders as he heads over towards the door.

I know he's being protective of me and I don't sass him. I pull my shirt over my head and he opens the door once I'm decent. He blocks my view of whoever is on the other side, but I hear them say, "Meeting in the conference room."

Ace nods and closes the door. He crosses the room and grabs a clean shirt out of his dresser and pulls it on. He grabs his socks and boot and pulls them on quickly before placing a kiss on my forehead. "We'll continue tonight." He promises, but I know he might not be able to keep the promise. I've lived my whole life with SEALs who get called out on missions at the drop of a hat. The same can be said about his job.

Chapter 11: Ace

I head down to the conference room. I wanted to stay wrapped up in Joanie now that I have Ghost's permission to date her. I just want to explore what I've been keeping myself from exploring every night when she crawls into my bed.

As I open the conference room door, everyone is waiting. At one end of the conference table, sits Viper and Cynthia. She's got his hand in a death grip. Sitting next to them are two men in suits and immediately I recognize one of them. They're FBI agents. If Cynthia is in this meeting, it means she's about to tell her story about witnessing a murder.

I take a seat, being the last man to enter the room. The agents take the lead in this meeting. It shocked Cynthia to learn the man she was messing around with while in captivity was an undercover FBI agent. I watch her intently, making sure she doesn't need medical attention.

The FBI agent informs us the man, Mr. Juarez, we arrested a few months earlier, has confessed to his part of the human slave trade. He's even admitted to giving the order to execute the man with whom Cynthia was having sex with, simply because she was being selective in who she was having sex with. But, since the execution took place outside the United States borders, the man who carried out the execution can't be prosecuted in the United States. The thought crosses my mind I won't be spending tonight with Joanie. *Fuck.*

I'm relieved to find out the FBI isn't going to hunt down his murderer right now. Their focus is on some new intel Mr. Jaurez gave them in trade for a softer sentence for his part in human trafficking. It's a group of men and women that work to convince young people to come with them into a club, more of a cult, that will accept them as they are. It's a good cover. The young people don't realize what they're getting into. Some are coerced into becoming prostitutes, drug dealers, or even sold without their knowledge into a life of what Cynthia just escaped.

The FBI is hiring us to infiltrate the group and cut the head of this snake off. The only knowledge Mr. Juarez gave them was the group is here in the Fort Hood area. Now the job for us is to find out where they are picking up these young, vulnerable people.

Viper shakes hands with the FBI agents and they head out the door after they again thank Cynthia for helping them close their fellow agent's case. Once the agents have left, we all begin tossing around ideas about where this group would pick up vulnerable people. We've got some good ideas about places where cults usually pick up their 'victims'. It's the next thing that's said that sends ice through my veins.

"We could let Joanie loose on the town and see where she would go. I mean, she's the perfect age, and she is known to make irrational decisions." Razor suggests.

I'm not about to allow *my woman* be used as bait. If we lost track of her, she could be lost for years and hell, I saw the results of what happened to both Viper and Cynthia. I sure as hell wouldn't survive the torture Viper did.

"She's still got a month or so in school." Viper says.

I don't like the tone in his voice. It sounds like he's considering what Razor suggested. My blood is running cold and I'm going to puke if they ask me to suggest this idea to Joanie. I feel my stomach roiling when I hear Zeke suggest, "We could put a chip in a phone before we give it to her to track and record everything. It would be how we keep her from being snatched."

OMG. These guys are actually considering using MY WOMAN! I stand up and head out the door. Running for the nearest exit, I head out the sliding door and onto the patio where I puke. I feel the warm air of the morning hitting my nostrils as my head finally stops spinning.

I feel a hand on my back. "Are you okay, son?" Annie asks.

I shake my head. We don't go into details about what's said in the conference room unless Viper gives us the go ahead. But just the thought of using her daughter as a piece of bait makes my stomach roll again.

Once I've gotten my stomach underneath me, I head back into the conference room. I've concluded that my brothers are delusional, and I'm the only one that will stand up for Joanie.

When I enter, the men are all huddled around discussing where to first try luring the men responsible for attracting these vulnerable young people. They've written different locations and they're talking strategy about scoping the locations out before bringing Joanie into the mix.

There are a good ten locations that the guys want to scout out. It'll take us weeks before having Joanie join us. When I open my mouth to protest, having Joanie join what comes out utterly surprises me.

"I'm Joanie's man in the field. If we're going to use her, I'm in the field with her." *What the fuck did I just say? Am I really contemplating letting the guys use Joanie as bait?*

"I wouldn't have it any other way." Viper replies to me.

If he could have been there with Cynthia when she was abducted he would have given anything to prevent it. So, he knows exactly how I feel at the moment.

"Razor will be your secondary, since he doesn't look like he poses a threat." Viper continues.

He points out several locations for Zeke and Hawk to start surveillance on. Several of them are local clubs, a few are parks near the base and bus station. Young, former military members who've recently been discharged are also a good target, as they are often depressed right after discharge and looking for what to do next. High schools are another good target ground for this group where they can troll the outcasts, like Joanie. That's why it really makes sense to everyone we are going to use her. Even if I don't like it in my gut.

When the guys leave the conference room, Viper pulls me aside and says, "I know you really don't like the idea of using Joanie, but it's really the best option we have. All of us look too confident to pass off the fact that we are vulnerable. Talk it over with her and help her understand. We'll invite her into the meetings as we narrow down the plan of attack closer to mission day."

I nod my head, not liking what I'm about to have to convince my new girlfriend to do in helping the team. Hell, I just got permission to date her and now I've got to convince her to be bait for a mission for our team. This is screwed up on so many levels. I just want to go acquaint myself with my girlfriend right now. I'll worry about the other later.

Chapter 12: Joanie

After his meeting, Ace came back in a weird mood. But around me, he's always been a bit weird. I guess that was because he was keeping his distance and trying to fight our attraction.

My dad headed back to San Diego on Sunday morning. Giving Ace another warning not to hurt me. Which, of course, Ace promised not to. After dad left, Ace turned the rest of the day into moving my stuff into his room. He used the excuse of not wanting me to feel as if I needed to sneak into his room anymore.

I feel as if he's skipping the whole courting step and jumping straight into the moving in together. Mom doesn't seem phased by his actions and actually helps us move my stuff into his room. *What the fuck is going on?*

Before I know it, Monday morning is here, and Doc is at headquarters to see me. I didn't realize I'd feel this nervous about spilling my history to a doctor. He's a nice older gentleman, and he takes copious paper notes. He asks me a ton of questions about my sexual history, medication I'm currently taking, and if I've ever been pregnant.

I answer them all, even as embarrassing as they are. Ace has asked me if I want him or my mom in the exam room with me during the procedure and, for the first time in my life, I really want my mom. She's a woman, and she's been through this before.

He waits until I've undressed and covered up with the blanket before he brings my mom into the exam room. She's confused as hell why I'm having a pap done, but she's happy I've chosen her to be with me. I'll have to explain to her afterwards what's going on, but for now I just need her moral support.

She holds my hand as doc does the procedure. Ace acts as his nurse, handing him the vials and equipment he needs. It feels good to have both Ace and my mom in the room. They both care about me. Doc leaves to pack the samples and allow me to redress.

When Doc comes back in, he sits on the rolling stool and addresses me. "Well, young lady, as far as I can see, the reason for your concern is valid, but not caused by any of the issues Ace and I thought it might be. We're going to have to wait for the results of the smears, but I'm thinking there's something more going on."

My mom looks between me, Ace, and the doctor. She's so in the dark about why the doctor is here. My mom finally asks, "Um. Excuse me, but exactly what are we talking about?" She's not mad, for once.

I motion for the doctor to give me a minute to explain what is going on. "Mom, I asked Ace the other day if it was supposed to hurt during sex. He went through some questions about sex with me and decided I needed to see the doctor."

Mom looks like she's going to get pissed at whoever has been having sex with me. But she also realizes that Ace and I weren't lying to her, we weren't sneaking around behind her back having sex. We were only seeking comfort in each other's arms at night. "I see." She says. "Why didn't you ask me before now?"

I hang my head and answer her. "Mom, we kept arguing, and I didn't want to seem like I was disappointing you. I'd had sex a few times with a few boys and each time it was painful."

The look on her face softens. "Babe, I would have let Dutch's wife talk with you if you needed questions about sex answered. Hell, I'm a romance author, but I don't know everything about sex. Your uncle Renegade and his wife had issues before they had their first child. She could have checked you out and helped you."

Doc clears his throat and says, "Ace and I thought it necessary to check her for endometriosis, fibroids, and uterine cysts. Those were the most common things he couldn't rule out without an examination of why she was having pain during sex. But after my examination, I didn't see any of the telltale signs of these problems." He pauses, studying both me and my mom.

"Now I won't be one hundred percent certain until I get the smear results. But I'm pretty certain something else is going on. I'd like her to talk to a friend of mine who is an OB/GYN. There are other reasons a lady has pain during sex. But, as far as I can tell, Joanie doesn't have any of the physical reasons." He pulls out a pad of paper and scribbles the doctor's name and number on the paper.

My mom asks, "Could she talk with a friend of the family that's also an OB/GYN and has worked with reproductive issues?"

Doc seems to consider it for a moment before he answers her. "I tell you what. I'll still give you this doctor's number. You can ask your friend, but if she says no because of a conflict of interest, then you'll already have my referral." He hands me the paper.

After the doctor leaves, I'm still worried about trying to have sex again and if it'll be painful. I've taken the day off of school work to process everything and thankfully the doctor gave me a doctor's note. Not like I really needed it since I'm ahead on my schoolwork. Ever since I got here, I've been completing extra work on the weekends, since I can't go anywhere without guards watching my every move. I've been keeping to myself and working on schoolwork. I have to attend classes for just over a month, but mostly, I've gotten two weeks ahead in the online work.

Ace picks up on my worry and shows me the medical page he used to help him talk to Doc about my issue. He goes through the medical conditions and eliminates them, even the ones Doc tested me for today. Then he scrolls down and I couldn't believe some things they listed for reasons to have pain during sex. I look through them.

"I've never had surgeries or other medical treatments down there, and no one has ever raped me." I say to Ace. but then my eyes land on the next two reasons listed. One is stress and the other is psychological issues. When I read through all those reasons, it's like I'm making a check mark over everything.

As I think back, every time I had sex, I wanted to anger my dad, but it always scared me we'd might get caught or I'd wind up pregnant and my parents wouldn't like the father of my baby.

Ace breaks through my thoughts and asks, "Hey Jo, what's going on in there?"

"I just think I've blocked myself from being able to enjoy sex."

"Do you want to talk to your mom's friend? Or do you want to talk to the doctor that Doc referred you to?" His hand gently rubs up and down my knee, causing goosebumps to rise all over my body.

I shrug, not knowing what I need to do. "I don't know. But the one thing I know is I'm not going to rush in and have sex. That's the one thing I've done with all my other partners. I've never really dated them, got to know them."

Ace nods as if he understands what I'm saying on a higher level. He asks me the weirdest question next. "Do you want me to get tested?"

"What? For what?"

He smiles at me. "Babe, I'm thirty-one. I've been with other women, and as much as I'd love to say, every time has been with protection, it hasn't. I'll get tested before we have sex, so you know I'm clean." I must be staring at him like he's speaking Russian because it causes him to chuckle.

I didn't realize how old he was. I knew he was older than me, but thirteen years. Damn, he could have fathered someone when I was still in elementary school. I say, "You'd do that for me?"

"Jo, I'd do anything for you." He answers me. "Moving you into my room isn't trying to control you, it's I want to see how we both sleep when we sleep the entire night together. It doesn't mean we have to have sex right away, it'll happen when you're ready." Ace gives me a kiss before he heads out to work on my parent's house.

It feels so good to kiss him. I get wet just from the passionate kiss. I'm happy for the first time in a long time. After what he said, he's willing to wait for me to be comfortable before we have sex. It makes feel warm and bubbly inside that this man would wait. None of the boys I've been with before have even suggested waiting.

Chapter 13: Ace

It's been two days since Joanie saw the doctor, and as promised, I'm letting her decide when we have sex. I've slept better the past two nights, having gone to bed with her. Her sweet scent is all over my bed and I wake up with a morning wood so hard I could prop myself up on it.

While I was working at the building site, Viper approached me and asked if I'd talked to Joanie about working on the undercover project. I haven't. He's pushing me to hurry up and get her on board.

I'm frustrated when I walk into my room after working all day on Ghost's house. It's coming along nicely, but now the plans have changed. Once Ghost's place is finished we'll start working on Viper and Cynthia's house since she's expecting twins in a few months.

I pull my dirty shirt off, throwing it into the hamper and lean down to untie my boots. Joanie isn't in the room, but she was at the build site, so I figure I'll hop in the shower before heading down to dinner. I finish striping off my clothes and tossing them into the hamper.

Stepping into the bathroom, my eyes land on my beauty. Joanie beat me up here and jumped into the shower. In the few days we've been dating, I haven't seen her totally naked. I open the clear shower door and slide in behind her. She lets out the cutest squeal when she feels my hand on her. My cock grows hard just hearing her squeal.

I can't help it. I want to touch her all night. My hands find her breasts and enjoy the way they fill them. She's not small breasted, nor is she large breasted. They're a medium size, but perfect for me. I pull her ass into my pelvis as my right hand wanders down her belly to her pelvis.

She takes in a gasp of air as realization of where my hand is about to go. My finger tips trail down her hip towards her mound. I feel her relaxing in my grip.

I slide my fingers over the seam of her lips. I can feel the flood of her juices at just the light touch. She's already wet, and not from the shower water.

I part her lips with two of my fingers and gently slide one of them inside. She's warm and tight around the one digit. If she's this tight around my finger, I can only imagine what she's going to be like around my cock. I nip on the lobe of her ear and whisper, "You ready for more?"

All Joanie can do is nod against my shoulder. "Good, because I'm going to make you come on my hand and then I'm going to take you to our bed and taste you. You're going to come on my face, and maybe if you're up for it, you'll come on my dick."

Jo moans for me as I pull the one digit out of her entrance and prepare to push the two fingers in together. As I do, her moan gets louder. Gently, I push and pull my fingers in and out of her channel. She coats my fingers in her juices. She rocks her hips in motion with my hand and I add my thumb to the mix, using it to rub on her clit and provide the pressure she's seeking.

Her walls grip down on my fingers and I can tell she's so close. I tighten my grip around her, not wanting her to fall. Then I speed up my assault on her pussy, thrusting my fingers in faster and harder. Jo shudders, squeezing on my fingers so tightly. Her body goes limp and I pull my fingers out of her tight cunt as her walls relax.

I hold her as the last of her orgasm passes. Our water has turned cold so I turn off the water. I wrap her up in the towel and walk her to the bed where I intend to do just as I told her earlier. Her legs still don't want to move her body right as I walk her to the bed, so she's at my mercy.

I lay her down on the bed and kiss her lips slowly, tenderly, allowing our bodies to touch completely. While she continues to recover, I run kisses over her jaw to her earlobe, down her neck to her collarbone and to her breast. At her breast, I take my time sucking and licking on each nipple until the bud is nice and pert.

My tongue finally takes the long path from the valley between her breasts down to her belly button. She squirms in anticipation of where my tongue is heading next. I stop for a moment and take a deep inhale of her scent.

Taking each of her lips under each of my thumbs, I spread them open and begin my languid assault on her. My tongue darts into her entrance each time I am at the bottom of her slit. As I approach the top, I flatten out my tongue to apply pressure to her clit. Joanie tries to close her legs around my head, but I don't allow it. I move my hands to her thighs and apply just enough pressure to fight her from closing her legs.

By the time I'm done, she's moaning and writhing on the bed, grabbing for anything to hold on to. I bet no guy she's ever been with has ever pleased her in the way I've just done. I want to sink my cock into her, but with the pain she's had in the past, I want it to be her decision to try.

I crawl up on top of Joanie and as I kiss the nape of her neck I ask her, "Do you want to try?"

She moans at the kisses I'm giving her and says, "Yes, because if I don't give it a try, I'll never try."

I reach over to my nightstand, but her hand stops me. "Don't, I want to feel all of you."

Fuck that's the sexiest thing any woman has ever said to me. But I don't want to risk getting her pregnant before she possibly goes on the mission Viper wants her to work on with us.

"I'll pull out then." I state acknowledging her want not to use protection.

"Please don't." She pleads with me, her eyes do me in.

I nod in recognition of what she's said. Knowing Ghost is probably going to kill me if she gets pregnant before we decide what it is we've got, but I know she's my soulmate. I would give my life to let her live.

I push just the tip inside her channel and damn, is she tight. The velvet feel of her walls squeezes on me and I watch her face for any sign of pain. Pulling back out and pushing myself back in just a little further than I had been the stroke before.

Joanie had been right. Penetration wasn't her problem. By the time I'm in all the way to the base, she hasn't shown any sign of discomfort. I move in slow, tender strokes, allowing her time to not only enjoy our love-making, but to give her what she needs a slow, intimate session. Not what she's used to; a quick let's get it over with fucking.

I could get lost inside of this woman. Everything feels right with her. Before I know it, her walls are clenching around me and she's arching her back up to greet me with every stroke. I know she's about to have another good orgasm. My balls tighten knowing she's about to come on my dick and I'm going to get the pleasure of coming inside of her. I speed up the pace and we come together.

I collapse on the bed and pull Joanie into my arms. I'm still seated inside her as my cock is softening. "Did it hurt?" I ask her. It's my first concern. Not if she enjoyed sex, but if I hurt her.

"No. It's the first time I've ever been able to enjoy sex," Joanie says, as she props herself up on one elbow and starts drawing little designs on my chest.

"Good." I say as I run my hands through her rainbow colored hair.

"You know, you're the largest man I've ever been with. I figured it would hurt; that the penetration would hurt."

I have to admit that's a bit of an ego booster. But what makes me smile most is the fact she was expecting some pain when I penetrated her, and it didn't hurt. I still have to talk to her about the mission that Viper wants her to work with us on.

I clear my throat and say, "Joanie, there's something I need to talk to you about."

"What's that?"

She's still drawing designs on my chest, and it feels so good. "Well, Viper and the team seem to think you're the right person to help us on a mission."

"On a mission!" There is excitement in her voice.

God this is not the reaction I was hoping for. "Yeah. I can't tell you much about it now, except you would be the lure for us to capture the criminals."

"That's cool. I'd love to help." She's bubbling over with excitement.

"It'll be awhile. The team has to do some research and put together a mission plan before we know when and exactly what your role is."

"Okay, that's cool." She says she's still excited. I'm still not excited about her participating on a mission. Well, that's a load off my chest since she's okay with participating on the mission.

Chapter 14: Joanie

When I woke up the next morning, I couldn't wait to talk to my friends at school. Ace had made love to me and held me for the rest of the night. For once, sex hadn't hurt. I log in for my first class of the day. I'm a few minutes early, and the teacher allows us to chat in the class chat before class starts.

Angel, one of my other best friends, notices I'm super excited today. Not normal for me here recently. She and Jen both also notice the change in my background.

Jen writes, "So what did you do, break another rule and dad committed you? And what drugs do they got you on to have you so chipper?"

"No, I changed rooms."

"What's up with all the masculine decorations?" Angel asks. She's noticed Ace's military awards hanging in the background, and some of the gear that's laid on the counter.

"Oh, they're Ace's."

"Who's Ace?" Both girls type in chat.

"My boyfriend." I type back.

"Wait! You got a boyfriend. I thought you weren't allowed to leave the headquarters." Angel types.

"I'm not. He works for N.R.T." I tell them.

"How old is he? There's no way for him to be your age." Jen types back.

"He's not, he's older."

"O.M.G. girl, your parents are going to kill you." Jen types.

"No, he asked dad if it was okay if we dated and dad approved of it." I explain to them. But class starts before I can tell them I've been asked to participate in a mission. Just as class starts, both girls send me wow emojis.

I live on cloud nine for the rest of my senior year. No more fighting with my mom, and I've even finished up my work for the end of my semester two weeks before the end of term. My teachers even notice an improvement in me and comment on it several times before the end of the year.

With Ace's encouragement, I've applied to the local community college to start in August. I'm pretty sure I want to go into EMT/paramedic for my major, but like everything else in my life, I'm unsure how it will turn out and how my parents will react if I back out of it. However, that's the last thing on my mind tonight. I graduate on Saturday and Ace asked permission from my mom to take me out to dinner tonight, as a celebration. To top it all off, he wants it to be a real date, the kind where he picks me up. It's a Thursday night, but with the rest of the high schoolers graduating either on Friday evening or over the weekend, he wanted to avoid the crowds and celebrate ahead of the ceremony, which I'll be attending via the internet.

I'm getting dressed up tonight. I'm wearing a dress I ordered online with Ace's credit card. The benefits of dating an older man, they have experience in bed and they have credit cards they'll let you use if you're responsible with it. It's a dark blue form fitting dress that doesn't go over my shoulders, it leaves them exposed. The bottom of the skirt on the dress comes about halfway down my thigh and I know I'll get laid tonight. Not that I don't get laid just about every night.

Ace and I have sex just about every night, but it's not sex, we make love. Sex with him doesn't hurt. He's slow every time we have sex, like he wants it to last forever. I don't mind, the three guys I had sex with before him wanted to hurry up and get the deed done so not to get caught by my dad or someone else. So it was quick, rough and with a condom on. The condom seemed to dry me out to the point I couldn't enjoy sex. That's why with Ace I asked him not to use a condom, and he's been very sweet about not pushing the issue. I know we're risking getting me pregnant, but I've never felt so right with someone in my entire life. But with Ace, everything feels perfect.

I hear him whistle as he closes our room door. "Mmm mmm mmm. You look yummy. I might have to skip on dinner and have my dessert first." He says as he wraps me up into a loving hug.

He's dressed in one of the other guys' rooms after work, so I wouldn't know what he was wearing. But he's looking sharp tonight, so I know I'm not overdressed for our date. I give him a quick kiss and then reach for my new shoes. They're black flats. It's the dressiest shoes I'll wear. Blame my dad for making me always be prepared for a situation that will probably never happen. I always want to run if need be. I don't want to be that woman in a horror film wearing high heels trying to run away from trouble falling and twisting my ankle while the pursuer approaches and eventually getting caught by her attacker.

"I'm ready to go whenever you are." I tell Ace.

He takes my hand and leads me down to the parking area. We approach a metallic blue crew cab Chevrolet truck. It's beautiful and looks roomy. He definitely needs the crew cab if he uses his truck for a work mission. Ace opens the passenger door and helps me into his truck.

The seats are also top of the line, two-tone black and grey leather. And the inside is nice, it even has a wireless charger for our cell phones, which I still haven't gotten back yet. Which means I can no longer give the excuse of my phone died and I didn't have a charger handy. The radio has a built in GPS, cameras that we can access, and even Ace has control over the different type of terrain and how the truck handles it. This truck is awesome.

Ace climbs in and we head out for my first time outside of headquarters since I arrived a few months ago. I'm both excited and nervous. I want to prove to my mom that she can trust me, but I also want to explore the town and see what all I've been missing out on.

He drives us into town and to a restaurant that isn't too classy, but isn't too casual. Ace has dressed in a pair of dress pants and a button-up shirt, leaving the top two buttons undone. He helps me out of the truck and up to the door where he tells the hostess his name and she immediately shows us to a booth near the back of the restaurant. The lights are low in the whole restaurant and it makes the whole setting intimate.

Ace orders a beer and I have a glass of water with dinner. I'm not big on sugary drinks. From the way the waitress looks at us, I can tell she's trying to decide if we're a couple or father and daughter. Ace sets her straight by taking my hand in his and kissing my knuckles lovingly. Not the way a father would do a daughter.

We eat our meal and enjoy a light conversation. I learn that Ace's real name is Noah Stone. That was the name he used to check in with the hostess. He's just gotten so used to answering to his call name he hardly ever answers to it.

As we are walking to Ace's truck, a group men surround us. My heart races at the way the men are looking over me. Ace pulls me behind himself and under his breath he says, "If things turn bad, hop into the truck, lock the doors, and drive like a maniac until you get the cops' attention." I can't believe he's telling me to leave him surrounded by several men if he gets into a fight with them.

"Hey old timer, we just want to introduce ourselves to the beauty you've got there." The first guy says, as he saunters closer toward Ace. He's a young hispanic guy barely out of high school.

I feel Ace slip the key to his truck into my hand as we take a step backward, closer to his truck.

"My brother just wants a little taste. You can go on your way." The second guy says. He's a black guy a bit older than the first one, maybe in his mid twenties.

Ace doesn't show his cards and announce that he's a SEAL. He just says, "You boys might want to rethink your target. Her father has entrusted her in my protection."

"What are you, Chuck Norris?" The third guy scoffs. He's the oldest looking and white. He also looks like he could do some damage to me if I was alone.

I feel the truck at my back and I hit the unlock button. Opening the door, I jump in and quickly hit the lock button as soon as I've closed the door. Just like Ace has ordered me to do. He's pinned up against the truck, and I fight the urge to open the door and pull him inside. He's taller than me and I would have to climb over the center console and with it having the gearshift closer to the passenger side, it makes maneuvering me and him around the gearshift even more difficult. I press the start button to start the engine and wait. Hoping Ace can talk the men down.

I'm unable to hear what exactly is being said, but I see the three men all pull knives, and I feel myself panicking. Seeing Ace fighting with the men who have knives, I remember exactly what he told me to do. I pull forward over the curb and into the roadway. As I speed off, I hear several car horns honking at me and I am sure someone has called the cops on me by now.

In my brain, I can hear Ace telling me to get as far away from where he and the men were fighting. But I love the man. My heart won't let me leave him there to possibly die. I turn the truck around after only driving down the main strip about half a mile, still trying to get the attention of the cops, but now I'm frantically trying to get back to him before he's killed. When I look up at the rearview mirror, I see the one button that I should have used earlier.

I reach up as I'm driving and press the button. I swerve to right myself in my lane. I've only driven a little and usually it's with my mom in the car with me. I only had gotten my license over the summer, but haven't really driven by myself since. Plus, mom wouldn't let me take my hands off the wheel to mess with the radio or my cell phone when I was learning to drive. So reaching up to press the button I over corrected, making me swerve. Now I just pray that Ace got the service when he purchased his truck.

"Roadside assistance. How may I help you, Mr. Stone?" A man's voice come's across the speakers as I'm turning back into the parking lot.

"Um, I need help. He's been involved in a fight." I say, trying to keep the panic out of my voice.

I look around and I finally find where we were parked earlier. The spot is still empty and Ace is laying sprawled out in the space.

"Ok. Ma'am, I've got your location. Are you okay?" The man's voice asks.

"Yes. He made sure I was in the truck before the guys attacked." I say, and I can hear my voice wavering as the realization of the moment hits me.

"Ma'am, I've got paramedics and police en route. Stay in the vehicle with the doors locked until they arrive." The man's voice is calm.

He tells me to put the truck in park, and to turn off the vehicle, after I've explained to him all the events that have happened before I hit the roadside assistance button. I do as he says while I keep my eyes on the parking lot. I watch Ace's breathing and with the dark of night, I can't tell what is blood and what is asphalt. Maybe that's a good thing.

When I finally see a set of emergency lights pull up behind me, I inform the man from roadside assistance. He refuses to get off the line until the officer identifies himself and he logs it into their records.

The officer knocks on my window, one hand on his sidearm and the other goes back to his belt as he steps back when I open up the door. He speaks with the roadside assistance person for a moment and then he helps me out of the truck and back over to his squad car.

He opens up the back passenger door for me and helps me to sit down. "This is for both of our protection, young lady." The officer says as he closes the door and his focus changes to where the injured man lies.

I watch as he turns on a small flashlight and walks over to where Ace lays. It's the first time I see the pool of blood. The officer speaks into his radio and before long, and I see an ambulance roll up with its emergency lights on. I try to open the door to climb out and rush over to Ace, but I can't open the door. It's child safety locked. I bang on the window in my frustration.

The officer and one paramedic come over to the car. The officer opens the door, and I try to bolt to where Ace is being treated by the other paramedic. Only I'm caught by both the paramedic and the cop.

"Woah, young lady. Let the paramedics treat your friend." The officer says as he tries to calm me down. I don't realize I'm shaking.

He wraps me up in his uniform jacket before he begins questioning me about what happened.

"I'm officer Sanchez. What's your name?"

"J-Joanie." I answer him. I'm still shaking, hard to believe on such a warm night I'm shaking like a leaf.

"And the gentleman over there, how do you know him?"

"Ace, he's my boyfriend." Officer Sanchez scribbles down what I've said before he asks his next question.

"Is he in a gang? I mean no offence, but the name Ace isn't exactly a real name, it's more of a nickname from a gang. Do you know his real name?"

"Ace is his call sign. He's a former SEAL." I pause, trying to remember Ace's real name since I've always called him Ace. "S-Stone, N-Noah." I finally stammer out.

Officer Sanchez nods and jots down the name I've given him. "Can you tell me what happened here tonight?"

I give officer Sanchez a rundown of what happened when we were heading to the truck. How Ace made sure I was protected and told me to run if things got bad. A few times during my explaination of the events, officer Sanchez has to tell me to slow down and calm me down. The whole time, I can't take my eyes off of what the paramedics are doing with Ace. They've got an IV in him and bandaged his wounds as best I can tell from here with all the flashing lights. As I watch them prepare to put him on their gurney, officer Sanchez says, "One more question and I'll let you ride to the hospital with your boyfriend."

"Were the men black, white, or latino?"

"All three."

Officer Sanchez notes my answer and then helps me over to the ambulance before he says, "I'll move the truck into the parking spot. Get yourself checked out at the hospital too. An officer will be in touch with you shortly, and they'll bring you the key." He hands me a card with a case number on it.

The paramedic takes over from there. I'm still shaking as he helps me into the rumble seat and buckles me in. Of course, the whole what's his name, what's your name, all begins again. I'm in such a daze that I answer the questions without realizing what the paramedic is doing. Before I know it, we are pulling into the hospital and I watch as they pull Ace out of the ambulance and into an emergency room.

There the doctors go to work on Ace and I'm pushed off to the side until a kind nurse realizes I'm traumatized. She pulls me out of the room and takes me to another room where a doctor checks me out, not finding any wounds on me. They determine I'm just in shock and the nurse talks calmly to console me. The doctor orders me some medicine to help me sleep while they treat Ace. The nurse reassures me when I wake up she'll help me find where Ace is at and make sure I get reunited with him.

Chapter 15: Ace

When I awoke, I'm in a hospital room and my memory of the night before is still fuzzy. As my memories start coming back, I remember sending Joanie off while facing three men. The men had pulled knives on me. I reach over to my left side, and sure enough, my memories are correct. I've got bandages there. I try to shift in the bed and a zinger of pain shoots through my left thigh. Pulling the bedsheet back and moving the hospital gown I'm dressed in shows a large bandage on my inner thigh.

The memory comes back to me now. The men pulled knives as Joanie did what I'd told her to do. I'm outnumbered three to one, and they're armed with knives. While I fight off two of the men, a third one takes swings at me. Cutting my shirt on my left side. I knocked out one man and was fighting with the other two men when suddenly I felt a sharp searing pain in my thigh. One of the asshats had stabbed me in the inner thigh. Shortly after that, I'd passed out.

As I'm processing what happened, knowing Annie and Ghost are going to kill me for letting Joanie leave and putting her in more danger. She doesn't know how to get back to the headquarters. I'm sure wherever she drove to, she's scared.

There's a knock on my door, pulling me out of my thoughts. A nurse enters and checks on my wounds before she pops her head back out the door to my room. When she opens the door wider, Joanie comes in. She's still dressed in her dress from last night, except now she's wearing a police officer's jacket. The nurse leaves the room.

"What happened?" I ask her, still somewhat confused. I point to the jacket she's wearing.

She blushes and answers me, "Oh, I realized you had roadside assistance so I turned around and went back to the parking lot." She explains. "I couldn't leave you there alone and not knowing if you were okay."

"Well, I'm glad you did." I pull her in close to me and give her a kiss.

Before I can deepen the kiss, there is the sound of someone clearing their throat. My eyes dart to the door where now two men stand. They are dressed in slacks and button up shirts with ties. A third man comes in behind them, and Joanie pulls off the jacket she's been wearing.

"Officer Sanchez, I think I forgot to give this back to you last night." She says to him.

He takes his jacket and lays it across his arm. He introduces us to the detectives. Officer Sanchez hands my truck key to Joanie in exchange for his jacket. As he leaves, he says, "Good to see you feeling better." I don't know who it is directed to since I've been out cold and don't remember him. I assume it's aimed at Joanie.

One detective takes Joanie out of the room while the other one talks to me. I do my best to describe my attackers to the detective. He tries not to give away any of his suspicions about the guys that jumped me, but I can tell he has his suspicions to who the suspects are. I don't ask since I don't want to blow the N.R.T. mission in a few weeks.

Once I'm done with my description of the attackers and what all I can remember, the detective opens the door and slips out to where his partner is with Joanie. A few minutes later, Joanie and comes back into the room. The two detectives stay out for a few minutes and I know they're comparing notes, it's procedure. Joanie is biting on the inside of her cheek like she's nervous about something.

"What's wrong, Jo?" I ask.

"They want me to go to the police department and look through some books of mugshots to see if I can identify your attackers."

"Did you get a good look at them?" I run my hand up and down her arm, trying to calm her nerves down.

"Yeah, I described their clothes to the detective, and I think I could remember their faces."

"Then work with the cops and get these jerks off the street." I encourage her.

"Okay." She leans down and gives me a quick kiss on the lips before the two detectives come back into the room.

The detectives inform me they'll send someone with some photo arrays for me to look at soon, and that Joanie is going with them to see if she can identify our attackers. I wish her luck before they leave, but something doesn't sit right with me when she looks back at me and the detective has his hand on her elbow. There's something she's not telling me.

The next time a nurse comes into my room, I have her hand me my belongings. I fish through the plastic bag and find my phone. It's dead. *Fuck.* I need to get in touch with Viper so he doesn't go ballistic and Annie doesn't worry about where Joanie is at. Plus, I want someone there with her to make sure she's not railroaded by the cops.

Chapter 16: Joanie

As I left the hospital room, I didn't know when I would see Ace again. The detective that pulled me outside of Ace's room had been kind at first, having me rehash the events of last night. He's jotting notes down as I tell him about the events. When I get to the part about me leaving the scene and then returning a few minutes later, his eyebrows raise.

Oh, shit, what is he about to do? I wonder to myself as he allows me to continue my story. When I finish, he asks me to describe the three men. I tell him there is one latino, one white and one black man. They all are in their late teens to mid twenties if I had to guess. Plus, they were wearing purple bandanas on different parts of their bodies.

That's when he suggests I come to the police station to look through some photo lineups of criminals to see if I can spot the men. "I'm not sure. I'm supposed to stay with Ace. If my family comes looking for me and I'm not with him, it's his ass." I tell the detective.

The detective changes his tactics and says, "Well, young lady, here's the way I see what happened last night actually happening. You hired the three men to hurt or kill your boyfriend. When you left that was their signal. Now I don't know what he's done to you or why you don't think you can tell a police officer and get help, but when you returned, he was supposed to be dead and you were to look like the grieving girlfriend. Only your boyfriend gave the men a fight for their life and he survived." He pauses for a moment when the door to the hospital room opens and the other detective slips out for a moment. "So, you can either come to the station and prove to us you weren't in on the attack on your boyfriend, or I can charge you with fleeing the scene of a crime and attempted homicide."

"Okay, I'll go." I answer him, feeling pressured and hoping that the tears don't start falling before I leave Ace's hospital room.

When I entered the hospital room, I kinda fibbed to Ace why I was going to the police station and he encouraged me to help the police find out who had attacked us. I'm also worried about my mom. I was supposed to be home at midnight. I know she's out of her mind by now. We haven't called nor shown up. She's the type of woman that jumps to the worst-case scenario. The only thing is I don't know the number to N.R.T. nor did I ever memorize my mom's cellphone number. I always took for granted I would have my cellphone with me to get in touch with her.

The detectives escort me out of the hospital and to their car. It's a sedan that doesn't stand out from the rest of the cars in the parking lot. When they let me into the car, one sits with me in the backseat and the other drives. This doesn't feel like I'm going to the police station to identify my attackers. It feels like I'm going to the police station to be questioned and arrested.

A few minutes later, we are pulling into the garage of the police station and I'm helped out of the car. My backseat guest escorts me to the interview room, as it's labeled. While the driver takes his sweet time getting the photo books, they want me to look through.

"Joanie, do you want something to eat or drink?" The detective asks me.

It's only now I realize I haven't eaten since last night. "Please." I answer.

Now I'm alone with my thoughts while I wait on photos and food. I'm so fucking nervous. They threatened me to get me to come here and I want to cooperate, but I'm not really sure I'm going to find the pictures of the men that attacked Ace.

A few minutes later, the two detectives and another gentleman enter the interview room. One detective has a couple of binders, while the second one has a sandwich and a bottle of water for me. It's the third gentleman that I'm concerned about. He sits at the table across from me and he's got a manilla folder in his hand. The first detective puts down the binders on the table and I immediately open the top one.

"My name is detective Ramirez. I'm part of the gang unit." *Well, that explains why you're dressed in jeans and a tee shirt.*

As I flip through the first book, I'm noticing all the pictures are of men that appear to be in a gang. The bandana must have been the giveaway. They've narrowed my suspects down to gang members. Detective Ramirez pulls out a piece of paper from the manilla and says, "Looking over your statement from last night, and reading the detective notes from earlier today, I'd have to say this was a gang initiation."

I continue to flip through the book and try not to let on as to how nervous I am about the whole situation. My eyes land on one man's picture. He's a white man holding a set of numbers from his previous arrest. I point to the picture and say, "He's the white guy that initiated the attack."

Ramirez writes down the guy's number and allows me to continue to flip pages. As I flip the pages, I ignore the white men and focus more on the latino and black men. Right as I get to the last page in the book, I see a black man who looks a lot like the man who attacked Ace. We go through the process again.

I open the second book and start flipping pages, but all of these men are white or black. The latino men are too old to be the one involved in the attack. When I get to the end of the book, I close it and look at the three detectives and say, "The third guy isn't in here. I'm sorry."

Then Ramirez pulls a picture out of the manila folder and asks me, "Is this him?"

It's a crime scene photo of a dead latino kid. The kid that attacked Ace and me. I take in a shocked breath. That kid was alive less than twenty-four hours ago. I nod at detective Ramirez. That's when he says something I can't believe.

"Joanie let me tell you how I think this played out." He looks me dead in the eyes. He's so close I can smell the cologne he's wearing. Between the picture of the dead latino kid and his overpowering cologne, I can feel my stomach about to lose the contents, or lack thereof. "I think these three attacked your boyfriend on your orders, and when it didn't go as planned and your boyfriend killed the latino kid, you came back to make sure your boyfriend was dead only to find this boy dead. You put him into the back of your boyfriend's truck and drove him over to a back alley where you dumped his body like a piece of trash. Hoping that he would get picked up today with the trash and your crime would go undetected for a long time. Then you called the police to look like a victim of a crime to cover up your involvement. Only with this being a holiday week, the trash schedule was rearranged and the restaurant owner discovered his body this morning. "

"No, that's not it. I love Ace." I protest against the detective's false allegations. "Hell, I'm not even from here. I only moved here a few months ago. I don't know anyone here. As part of my punishment, my parents took away my cell phone and all internet access except to do with my schoolwork." I explain how there is no way I can be involved in the crime.

"So, you lashed out on the man who was your watchdog, not your lover." The detective says.

"No." I shake my head vehemently. "Ace and I fell in love, he asked my parents' permission to date, and we were out celebrating my graduation tomorrow...I mean today." I'm starting to hyperventilate I can't even keep track of the days anymore, let alone make a coherent thought.

I know I need to make a phone call and get Viper and or my dad involved, but for the life of me I can't think of any numbers right now. Suddenly, I realize that I haven't given them the biggest piece of evidence to prove that I'm not involved.

"I'm supposed to work with N.R.T. in a few weeks on a human trafficking case. Ace is with N.R.T.. Call. Viper. He's their leader."

The men get quiet and head out of the interview room and my once hungry stomach now feels like it's about to revolt. I'm angry these men think I could be cold enough to plan a murder. I grab the sandwich and throw it at the wall. Then I throw the water bottle at the wall too. I'm pissed. The water bottle hits a window in the wall and a few seconds later, an officer I've never seen before comes in and says, "Calm down, young lady. Or else I'll have to restrain you."

I know exactly what he's talking about when he says he'll restrain me. He'll cuff me to the table. It's obvious because there's a ring on the table for the cuffs to go through and the table is bolted to the floor.

"Fine." I huff out and start pacing the room.

The officer watches me tentatively for a while before he slips back out the door he came in. I continue to pace back and forth for what seems like forever. I'm wondering what is taking the detectives so long.

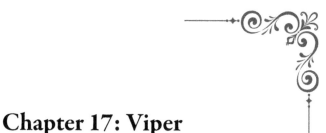

Chapter 17: Viper

I've been up since the crack of dawn with an anxious Annie. Joanie and Ace were supposed to be home by midnight. But they haven't shown up nor called to check in. It's not like Ace not to check in if he's going to be late or been held up. But I can't let Annie know I'm seriously concerned about Ace and Joanie's wellbeing.

I'm holding my second cup of coffee of the morning and I'm hovering over Zeke. He and Hawk are searching the local hospital and law enforcement for their names. So far, nothing. But the systems aren't updated with every entry. They're on a delay and as much as Zeke and Hawk know about hacking and not leaving a trace, they have to go with what's in the cloud.

Annie has called Ghost, and he's already on his way. He was going to surprise Joanie for her graduation, bringing Liam with him so they could do the ceremony together. But now I know he's panicking. His girl is missing in a city she's never been in before. My gut is telling me it has something to do with the human trafficking case we're working on, but I try to push it aside.

I try again to call Ace's phone. It goes straight to voice mail just like every time I tried to since about five this morning. Before that, the calls rang through and then went to voice mail. He's either turned off his phone or it died from all the calls and text messages I've sent. Plus, I'm sure Ghost and Annie are blowing up his phone, too. I'm going to kill Ace if he's curled up in a hotel room with Joanie safe and sound while me, Annie, Ghost and the rest of the team are worrying about them.

Razor brings me out of my thoughts when he says, "Viper, there's a detective Ramirez on the phone and he only wants to speak with you."

I look at him, confused. I know Ramirez. He's with the gang unit. Why's he calling me? We're not working on any cases together at the moment. I reach for the phone Razor is handing me and take it not so gently. I'm not in the mood for interruptions.

"Viper." I say bruskly.

"Viper, I think you might want to head your ass my way." Ramirez chuckles into the phone, trying to ease the tension.

"Why? I'm in the middle of something at the moment."

"Well, if it's what I think you're in the middle of, then our cases have crossed."

"You've got my attention."

"You're working on a human trafficking case, right?"

"How'd you find out?"

"Well, a little rainbow haired birdie told me."

"Joanie."

"Yup. Apparently, her and her boyfriend were attacked by some gang members and the detectives and myself read the whole situation wrong. But I really need you to come and fill in the blanks to verify her story."

"Shit. Where's Ace?"

"He's recovering in the hospital."

"Which one?"

"Killeen General."

"Thanks. I'll be at the station in an hour." I say, ending the call.

"Hawk, you and Razor go to Killeen General hospital and check on Ace. Zeke, you hold down the fort here while I'm gone to see what kind of mess Joanie has gotten into." I order my men as I head out to grab Annie.

I head up to Annie's room. I throw open the door without knocking and say, "I know where they're at." That's when I realize she's on the phone with Ghost.

"I'm gonna kill him if they're curled up in a hotel safe and sound." Ghost threatens through the speaker of her phone.

"Come on, Annie, I'll explain on the way."

Annie grabs her phone and purse. She promises to call Ghost when she has more information. While she's finishing up her conversation with Ghost, I pop my head in and tell Cynthia where I'm headed. She knows who to talk to if there's a problem with the babies, but I sure as hell hope there's never a problem.

We're almost out of the first trimester for both babies and she's finally getting some of her energy back.

I try to explain to Annie about the phone call I received from detective Ramirez. But the minute she heard the word detective come out of my mouth, Annie started asking me what Joanie had done to get into trouble. Now I know where Joanie gets her jumping off in the deep end from.

When we enter the police department, detective Ramirez greets us. He and I decide it's best for me to go into the interview room with Joanie since Annie is still a bit worked up. Ramirez shows Annie to where she can watch the interview with the officer who's been keeping an eye on Joanie while he and the other detectives were out of the room, per protocol.

Ramirez and I head into another interview room where he asks me, "What's this she says about working for N.R.T. on a human trafficking case?"

I nod and give him a brief rundown of the case we're working on with the FBI. I tell him where we suspect the people are being nabbed from and who are being targeted.

He explains about her and Ace's attack and how he and his fellow detectives thought she had hired someone to kill Ace. He even tells me about her leaving the scene per Ace's orders to get help, and how it looked as if she had returned to make sure Ace was dead. When she had mentioned N.R.T. Ramirez knew he could have my guys check her internet activity and verify she wasn't involved.

"I can do one better. We've been monitoring her internet activity since she arrived at headquarters."

"What about her cell phone?

"She doesn't have one. Her parents took it away when she came to headquarters." Ramirez nods at what I've said.

"Well, I think her cover is blown." Ramirez says.

"Why?" I ask him.

Ramirez shows me the two people she picked from photo arrays. Which he also had sent to the hospital and Ace also picked out of photo arrays. He explains the gang unit has been trying to figure out how one of the newest gangs on their radar Friends is making their money. He tells me the gang doesn't discriminate on race or sex. They let just about anyone into the gang. His unit hasn't been able to track down any links to drugs or other criminal activity.

When Joanie had mentioned the purple bandanas and Ace's state when he was taken to the hospital the detectives all thought maybe murder for hire was the way they were making money. Then Joanie mentioned human trafficking and our case. Everything started clicking.

He's right, if the Friends are involved, her cover could be blown. Since two of their members saw her, they could identify her and vice versa during our operation. I've got no choice but to pull her from the operation.

"Fuck! This screws up my whole sting operation. She's the only woman on the team."

"Not totally, my friend. Let's get Joanie settled down, and then I'll introduce you to a friend of mine, Beth Ann. She works with us occasionally."

I nod in agreement, and Ramirez shows me into the interview room where Joanie is being held. She looks like hell. She's pacing back and forth when we enter and doesn't see me. I wrap my arms around her, pinning her arms to her waist, and I whisper in her ear, "What did I tell you about scaring the shit out of your mom again?"

She pales, but she's also happy I'm in the room. "Viper!" She announces as she tries to turn around in my arms.

"Sit." I order her.

She does as I've told her to. I can see the nervousness in her eyes. She's got so many questions she wants to ask me, but she's ready to listen.

Chapter 18: Joanie

Viper showed up! Now maybe I can get the hell out of this trouble the cops have made up. I keep my mouth shut when he orders me to sit down at the interview table. At least he's not having detective Ramirez cuff me to the table.

Viper has me explain what happened last night and when I tell him Ace told me to leave, he understands why I left and then came back. Ramirez even tells Viper I've cooperated with the cops since they first showed up on the scene last night. I think I see a smile cross his face, but it's so hard to tell with his beard and his stone cold look.

"Why'd you feel it necessary to mention the mission with N.R.T.?" Viper asks me.

I shrug my shoulders. I had just blurted it out, hoping against hope someone would know about his team. "I don't know. I was being accused of setting up Ace to be murdered and disposing of the boy's body." I motion towards the picture of the dead latino boy still sitting on the table.

Viper's hand lands on mine and he says, "The cops were only exploring every option. They're doing their job. Trying to get the guilty to confess to their crimes." He moves the picture of the dead latino boy and turns it over so I'm not having to look at it constantly.

"I hope I didn't blow things for the mission." I say, apologetically.

"Well, you didn't intentionally." He says. "It just so happens that our case may have crossed paths with one detective Ramirez is working on, and if so, I can't use you and Ace as the primary targets." He explains to me.

"You can't use Cynthia or my mom." I argue. "Anyway, why are we having this conversation here? Am I free to go?"

"Yes, and No." Viper says.

"What do you mean?"

"Well, the officers aren't charging you with leaving the scene, since Ace told you to leave to protect you. But since the other two attackers saw you, detective Ramirez and I think it's best to keep you here in protective custody."

"What? You're going to lock me up like some criminal?"

"It's only for your protection. While we run the operation. Then we'll have you released." Viper tried to explain, but I was having none of it.

Ace is still in the hospital and is expecting me to return to him. And now Viper is telling me I'm going to be held in a cell against my will until he and the guys have run their mission. If he thinks I'm going to do this without a fight, he's got another think coming.

"I get that I've been spotted and that I'm not the type of person to blend in with the background Viper, but let me work the mission in some way." I beg him.

He shakes his head and says, "Ace is going to be in the hospital for a few more days, at least. And I can't risk you being seen with the rest of the crew and ultimately blowing our cover. I promise you I've weighed all the pros and cons of this decision. Your mom and dad are going to be pissed at me, but it's for the best."

"I promise I won't leave headquarters." I argue.

Viper lowers his head and shakes it. "No can do Joanie." Then he stands and heads towards the door where the officer earlier came through.

As he enters, I hear my mom laying into him, but the door closes before I can hear much more. Detective Ramirez touches my shoulder and says, "Come on, Joanie, we've got to make it look real for everyone involved."

I feel him gently tug my right hand behind my back and the cold metal of his handcuffs tighten down on my wrist. As he takes my left hand, the first tears slip down my face. I feel the handcuffs tighten down and detective Ramirez says, "Don't worry, I'll keep tabs on you and make sure you're okay."

It's not that I don't trust Viper's decision, it's the fact putting me in jail even though I really didn't commit a crime is going to be just as traumatizing as if I had been falsely accused of a crime and thrown into jail. I don't know how to express it in words to the detective as he walks me over to a desk to enter my information into a computer.

He pulls out a chair, and I sit down. It's uncomfortable metal and I'm forced to practically sit on my hands. I'm uncomfortable, angry and tired. Even though the doctor had given a sedative which had made me sleep deep and hard. When I'd woken up, I was still tired, as if I hadn't slept at all. It's as if detective Ramirez can read my mind and he says, "Look, Joanie, with you able to positively identify the attackers and two of them are still out there, your life is at risk. Now I've known Viper for almost four years, and if he thinks you're safer in a jail cell, then I have to go with what he says. Think of the latino kid, he was probably being initiated into the gang and because the initiation went wrong, they killed him." Detective Ramirez says, looking at me dead serious.

"They could kill you just because you saw them." He adds on under his breath. Sending a chill through me all the way to my bones. "With us putting you in PC and writing it up as if we don't believe your story, they won't be able to get to you in jail."

I finally find words to verbalize one of the many questions that are swarming through my head. "Won't the fact I'm in PC make the other inmates suspicious about me?"

"No, we always put violent offenders into PC for a period of time. It can vary from a few weeks to permanent." He explains.

"What about Ace?" I ask, having heard him refer to me as a violent offender.

"You murdered him." He says.

"What about the mission?"

Detective Ramirez smiles and looks just over my shoulder at someone. I want to turn around and see who he's looking at, but it would throw my balance off and I'd fall out of the chair, bringing the attention of everyone in here to our conversation. "Don't worry, I've helped the guys with a replacement for you." He says, before he turns the conversation back to preparing me for the whole booking procedure.

I can't help but be nervous about the whole being put in jail. I can feel my whole body shaking with nervousness. Detective Ramirez sits at his computer typing up his report. He's terribly slow, he's a hunt and pecker. God, I couldn't get a cop that can type thirty words a minute. My arms are falling asleep. Occasionally, he asks me a question as he continues to enter information into the form he's filling out.

Finally he prints out what he's been typing up and helps me up. We head down in an elevator to a basement level, it seems. Just standing up and heading down to the basement, I'm regaining the feeling in my hands again.

He leads me through a door that he has to use an identification badge on. We walk to a reception like desk and he hands the printout to the officer sitting behind the desk. The officer reads through the paper and says, "Anything to add?"

Detective Ramirez says, "Yeah, she's an IS-5."

I see the other officer raise his eyebrows at the statement and then he nods and says, "We'll take good care of her."

Ramirez takes the cuffs off and says, "Now follow these officers' orders. Don't talk to the other inmates, and when they allow you to make a phone call, pretend to. I'll send down someone periodically with information."

He signs the log book and turns and leaves. I'm scared witless at the moment. I know I've done nothing wrong, but to put me in a place with real criminals doesn't seem to be the best place to keep me safe.

A female guard comes around the desk and instructs me on the first procedures of intake into the jail. She explains to me this is only holding until I'm transferred to either prison or the county jail, whichever it is I've been assigned to go to. She places a grey container on the counter for me. She has me remove all my jewelry, then I'm told to take off my shoes. She hands me a pair of slippers to put on. I then have to grab the container and follow her as she leads me into a dressing area where I have to undress, including my underwear and bra. Once I'm naked, I'm instructed to shower and wait for the guard to inspect me for contraband. When the guard inspects me, I feel violated in the worst way. Her gloved fingers have been in every orifice I have. She's checking for possible contraband. Then I'm given a pair of white granny panties to wear, but not a bra.

She then hands me a set of what looks like oversized grey scrubs. I'm not a small woman, but I'm not huge and these things barely fit me. They hang down so far in the front I can feel the breeze between my breasts, and I'm constantly having to pull the bottoms up to keep my ass covered. I can only hope I'll be able to get another set at the jail that fits better.

When we get back out to the reception area, she takes me over to a desk and takes my picture, verifies all the information on my paperwork is accurate, and then takes my fingerprints via a digital scanner. Then she verifies the charges against me and informs me of my rights again. I sign a tablet that sends the signature to the computer. She prints out a copy of the updated information with my picture and everything on it and gives me a band like in the hospital with a scan bar and a picture matching me in the ugly grey scrubs.

She then leads me to a room and gives a pillow, a bag of toiletries, and a roll of bedding. From there, she takes me down a hallway and into a set of cells that sit at an angle from a watch desk at angles. Each little hallway has three cells on it, one on each side and one at the very end, so the officers at the desk can watch what's going on in each cell. Most of the cells have multiple inmates in them. We pass several of the hallways and go into the last one. Here the doors open to the cell on the left-hand side and I'm led into a cell with a single bed. This must be the isolation cells. Since there are more cells on this hallway and they are all single inmate cells.

I unroll the mattress that sits on the single bed, and make the small bed with the bedding I was given, and toss the pillow onto it. I put the toiletries in the small area for the bathroom in this cell. There is nothing to do in the cell, so I lay down on the bunk and try to sleep.

Chapter 19: Ace

I sleep thanks to the pain medication for what seems like days, only when I wake Joanie isn't there to greet me. It's my brothers Hawk and Razor. I'm still groggy when the doctor comes in and gives me an update on what they had to do to save my life. The stab wound hadn't penetrated my femoral artery, but it had come damn close. They'd had to stitch up several layers of muscle tissue. As for my side, I had several slicing wounds which they stitched up easily, but after the beating I'd been given I had bruises everywhere that needed to heal too.

When I ask Razor and Hawk where Joanie is at they try to avoid the question by telling me I'll see her soon enough. I know I'm in no shape to do our mission in the coming weeks, as my leg will take time to heal. I've already accepted I've been sidelined. I'm worried how Joanie is going to accept doing the mission with Razor and whoever Viper replaces me with. I want to talk with her and make sure she understands she's mine even if they have to act like a couple; it means nothing.

Razor and Hawk alternate shifts in my room while I recover. I am unsure how long I'm in the hospital, but I've not seen Joanie since she left with the two detectives. I don't know why Viper isn't letting Joanie see me, nor why these two knuckleheads are guarding me like my life is on the line.

Knowing the day for the mission is coming and I'm getting stir crazy I ask my watchdog, "Why aren't you at headquarters preparing for the upcoming mission?"

"You right now are my mission." Hawk says, not lifting his eyes from his phone.

"What do you mean?"

He huffs out a breath of air and puts his phone down. "Look, the guys who attacked you killed one of their own. And until the mission is over, it has been

83

deemed that you and Joanie need to stay put. So I'm here making sure you stay put."

"So, what Joanie is at headquarters and can't even call me?"

Hawk shifts in his chair and I know that body language from him. It means he's preparing to run if I don't like what he says next. "Well, no. That's not it. She's being held at the jail." He turns his phone and shows me the booking photo.

"What the fuck!" I'm ready to bolt out of the bed and attack my brother, except I feel the tug of the tube they stuck up my junk while I was knocked out. If it wasn't for that, Hawk would be running for his life with me chasing after him.

"Technically, for her protection, and yours, you're dead. And she's in jail for your murder." He explains.

All I can see right now is red. I know how jails are and Joanie isn't safe in a jail, hell she's probably in more danger there. The women in jail are crazy. You look at them wrong and they'll beat the shit outta you.

"How the fuck is she safer in a jail than at headquarters?"

Hawk shrugs. Apparently, he wasn't in on the decision behind putting my woman in jail. "Does Ghost know?"

"Yeah, he's not happy about the whole situation. He sent Liam back to San Diego after graduation and he's stayed at headquarters."

"Fuck." I mutter. This doesn't bode well for me. He's probably pissed that I got his little girl involved in all of this.

"Yeah, he's driving the rest of the guys crazy constantly asking questions, and wanting to do something, anything." Hawk admits.

He continues to fill me in on the goings on of headquarters to help with my being stir crazy. At least, until the nurse comes in to give me more pain medication. Once it hits, I'm out for a few hours, again.

Hawk even tells me about the woman they've replaced Joanie with on our mission. She's a young, blonde headed woman who looks younger than her age. She and Razor are taking the lead on the mission, since both Joanie and I are down. Apparently, Razor is smitten with her, but he's too ashamed of his disability to think a woman like her could look past it.

Razor lost his arm just below the elbow on a mission a few years ago. The Navy gave him a medical discharge, and he's been fighting with the VA to get a real prosthetic. The guys and I have gotten used to him walking around without his prosthetic at headquarters, but whenever someone new is around or we are on a mission, he straps on the prosthetic arm and won't take it off until he's in his room. It doesn't match his skin tone, nor does he have much control over what it does. But on the bright side he gets away with accidentally grabbing ass and not knowing it when we go to the bar.

I just want to snuggle next to Joanie and feel her body next to mine. Now that I know where she's at, I have to wait until the mission is over before I can hold her again. I'm going to make slow, passionate love to her when I get her back in my arms and my bed. For now, I'll have to let the dreams of us together suffice.

Chapter 20: Joanie

I must have dozed off in the small cell because I'm awoken by the cells near mine opening and an officer calling names. As I sit up, I see the other inmates lining up and being patted down and cuffed. I figure my time is coming. But my cell never opens, nor is my name called. I sit on my bunk for what seems like forever, as the process is repeated which I figure one was for the prison and the other is for the local jail.

I can hear several rowdy inmates, but they're not in my little hallway. As the time goes by, the sound gets quieter and I feel like I've been forgotten. Maybe they're not transferring me today. I really wish I had my watch or some way to tell time.

I sit on the bunk and think back to my conversation with detective Ramirez. He said he'd send someone down periodically with news. How can he do that if I'm in jail? The lady in intake said this was only a holding cell until they shipped me to the jail or prison. He must have left something out. I think back to what he said to the officer at intake, he said "I was an IS-5"and the guy's reaction was shocked, plus he said "they'd take good care of me."

The more I think about it, the more I'm thinking Ramirez and Viper left something out when they told me I was going to jail. I'm pulled out of my thoughts when I hear footsteps heading my way. I'm pretty sure by now it's just a guard with an inmate.

"Anderson, J." I hear the guard say. "Stand up, turn around and approach the door, placing your hands at the slot."

I do as the guard instructs me to do. I feel the cuffs tighten around my wrists and I steel myself to keep from crying. The door to my cell opens and I feel the guard take my elbow and lead me out into the hallway. I'm led back to the intake area and to where I had entered earlier. The guard hands me off to a female officer.

"Am I the only female being taken to the jail?" I ask the female officer as we exit the intake area.

Once we're out of the intake area instead of heading straight to the parking area, she pulls me to the left where the elevators are at. She presses the indicator button on the elevator and then moves behind me. Suddenly, I feel the cuffs release from around my wrists. I don't dare move my hands. I don't want the officer to accuse me of doing something I didn't do.

"No, you're not being taken to the jail, but I'll let detective Ramirez explain it to you."

I move my hands to my sides as the elevator doors open and we step inside. We ride up in a comfortable silence. When the doors open again, the floor is quiet and most of the lights have been turned off and most of the officers are gone. The officer shows me over to detective Ramirez's desk.

Ramirez isn't at his desk, but there is a change of clothes and some tennis shoes there for me. The female officer says, "I guessed at your shoe size." She points to the shoes sitting on top of the clothes.

I pick up the clothes and she shows me over to a restroom where I can change out of the jail clothes and into more human clothes. I'm confused about what's going on, but I'm going with the flow. When I go into the restroom, I find she's slipped in a pack of new underwear into the stack of the clothes and they're not the plain white granny panties, the jail issues they're colorful and hi cut, more my style. I'm thankful for these little things, even if I've only been in a holding cell for a few hours.

When I come out, she walks with me back to Ramirez's desk. Now he's sitting at his desk. "Thank you, Beth Ann." He says to her before she leaves.

He finally looks at me and says, "Sorry about the inconvenience, but we had to make it look as if you were in jail. You still have to stay hidden away, but it's too risky to take you to a safe house. So, you're going to stay here in the police headquarters until your guys take down the guys that we're sure are both involved in the sex trafficking case and the attack on you and Ace."

He explains that if the gang has been watching me since the attack intending to grab me, they've probably got someone watching the police headquarters, and with my picture going on the police website as being charged with the murder of Ace, it should be enough to keep them thinking I'm in jail.

"So, I'm on lockdown here in the police headquarters?" I ask.

"Unfortunately." He answers. "At least the bunks here are more comfortable than the ones in the prison."

He stands up and motions for me to follow him. I do, and he shows me into a set of rooms I hadn't seen before. Each room has a twin size bed, a nightstand and an area to place some personal items. Then he points out the restroom and showers. He promises to have Beth Ann bring me some shower items so I can feel human while I'm here.

Next, he takes me over to a little break room with a table. Sitting on the table are several takeout containers of the typical cop food, Chinese takeout, along with the officer that brought me up to this area, Beth Ann.

I had noticed earlier she was shorter than me, but I'm not the type to size a person up in order to fight them. A person's height means nothing as to their capabilities to do a job. Her hair is sandy blonde and she's wearing a pair of thick glasses. I notice she's not dressed like a uniformed officer nor like the detectives I've seen around here. She's wearing a dark blue polo shirt with the emblem of a badge embroidered on it and a pair of khaki cargo pants. No gun belt, cuffs, nothing like any normal officer.

"Joanie, I want you to meet Beth Ann. She's going to be taking your place on the mission the N.R.T. are running." Detective Ramirez says breaking me out of my thoughts.

"Hi." I say to Beth Ann, offering to shake her hand.

"Hi." She returns, meekly.

I turn to detective Ramirez and ask, "She's a cop. The men they're tracking surely have noticed her if she's here all the time."

Ramirez shakes his head and chuckles before he says, "She's not a cop. She's a civilian contractor with the department. She's everywhere and nowhere."

I must give him a confused look before she fills in for him, "I answer the phones, file paperwork, put together the mugshot books, volunteer to work undercover operations when there aren't female officers available, and I run paperwork to the courthouse when needed. I'm too blind to be a cop, so..." She shrugs. "I choose to help in the field I wanted to work in. People see me when they need to see me, but since I'm not in uniform, so to speak, they typically ignore me." The last piece was added with a bit of sadness.

"I'm sorry." I say, knowing the feeling of only being seen when I'm in trouble and not when I'm doing something right.

"Oh, don't be hun. It comes in handy from time to time. People see the glasses and just ignore me. I don't know if they think I'm a geek or I'm dumb. Either way, most don't want to talk with me beyond whatever interactions they *have* to do."

"Have you tried contacts?"

"Yeah, they don't feel right on my eyes. Anyway, I'm going to the N.R.T. headquarters tomorrow and I wanted to know if I could pick up anything for you to help with the boredom of being lockdown?"

"Yeah, could you bring me my tablet and my game system?"

"If it's a handheld game system, then yeah. Otherwise, I'm sorry I can't bring the big systems in here."

I explain to Beth Ann it's a handheld system full of my downloaded games. Also, I tell her who to speak to about getting my stuff. I'm surprised to find out she's already met my mom. While I was being arrested, she was talking to my mom, calming her down and introducing herself to Viper.

"Are all the guys with N.R.T. as handsome as Viper? I saw the wedding band and, well, I'm not the type of woman to go after a married man, but wow, he's hot!"

I chuckle because it's obvious detective Ramirez is feeling a little inadequate. Since he adds, "What, you're not surrounded by enough hot cops daily?"

Beth Ann and I both chuckle at his question and she answers back, "Most of you guys are married." She points to Ramirez's wedding band. "The others don't really notice me or we're just friends. It's nice to expand your horizons and possibly meet someone special."

Detective Ramirez nods at what she said, knowing she wants her own happily ever after. We eat the rest of the meal in a comfortable silence. When we're done, Beth Ann says her good nights and makes her way to the exit.

Ramirez makes sure I'm in my room before he escorts her out to the parking lot and then he comes back up to the officer's sleeping quarters. He knocks on my door before he pokes his head into the room and says, "I'm going to be just next door if you need anything."

"I thought you were going home." I state.

"Nope. I'm in charge of watching over you, so I'm staying here too." He informs me.

"Isn't your wife going to be upset?"

"No, she's used to the weird hours. Plus, I'll call her in a bit and talk to her before I fall asleep."

"No wacking tom tom. I don't want to hear your moans through the walls." I tease, trying to ease the tension between us.

Detective Ramirez chuckles at my attempt of a joke and says, "She's a nurse and she's at work, so not happening anyway."

I nod and then settle into my bed for the night. Thankfully, Beth Ann had given me a pair of sweatpants that fit me and a tee shirt. I turn off the light on the nightstand and close my eyes. It's been a rough day and sleep shockingly comes quickly.

Chapter 21: Ace

I am finally released from the hospital after a week and a half, but my guys don't let me leave. They still haven't run the mission. It angers me that Joanie is sitting in jail this whole time and they're drag assing. The guys inform me the mission is going down tonight. But I swear the hours tick by so slowly.

I want Joanie back in my arms, making passionate love to her. When I get back to headquarters, I'm going to hang Viper by his nuts for allowing Joanie to be locked up with real prisoners.

It's late when Hawk finally picks me up from the hospital. He explains on the ride home Viper and detective Ramirez's reasoning for keeping me and Joanie in the hospital or locked up. They suspect gang members we had tangled with that night to be in the same gang as ones involved in our human trafficking case. They were worried both the hospital and the police station were being watched and both our lives and the mission were in jeopardy.

I don't even wait for Hawk to finish parking his truck when I jump out and head inside headquarters. I've had plenty of time to think about some things and tonight I can't fix all of them, but the one I will fix is that when decisions about my woman are made from now on they will be run through me. No more putting her in jail and having me worried about her wellbeing.

"She's not in there, and neither is Viper." Hawk calls out after he finished parking and is jogging to catch up.

My strides slow down. Having heard the man I want to talk to isn't available. I turn and face Hawk. "What do you mean, he's not here?"

"The mission is wrapping up, but they gave me the all clear to bring you back to headquarters."

I try to temper my frustration. "I wish I could say I know how you feel, but I've never been overly infatuated with a woman before. I've kept them at arm's length and never let my heart get involved." Hawk says as we continue to walk into the headquarters.

I head straight to the refrigerator and grab a beer, then I pick up my mail. There's not much here for me except the usual bills letting me know how much they're pulling from my bank account for the next payment. I grab Joanie's mail next, she's only got a few letters. One of them is from the local community college, and another is from someone in San Diego.

I take my beer and the mail for Joanie and me up to our room. I plop down on our bed and I am surrounded by her scent. Frustrated, I finish my beer and head to the bathroom for a shower. I haven't had a proper shower since I was admitted to the hospital. The hospital shower didn't allow me the relaxation that my personal shower gives me. Plus, I wasn't allowed to get my stitches wet for several days, so it was several days before I even attempted a shower. I'm still sore, hopefully the shower will relax that out of my muscles.

I head into the bathroom and look in the mirror. Shit, my mohawk has really grown out. Before I even turn on the water, I reach for the hair trimmers and run them through my hair, shaving the sides down to the skin. That looks better, but I will need to hit the barbershop for a trim on the top soon.

Stepping into the shower, the water is scalding hot, just the way I like it when my muscles are tense and sore. The only thing that could help this pain go away other than the scorching hot water is Joanie. Being buried deep inside of her would make me relax, too.

I'm standing in the shower allowing for the water to run over my tightened muscles when suddenly behind me I hear a noise. Not a noise, more of a squeal. "Ow. Shit. That's fucking hot." It's Joanie. I immediately turn the water temperature down and turn around to wrap her up in my arms.

My cock reacts to seeing her naked in our shower. "It's about damn time." I say, as I examine her wrists for where the cuffs were at. There is no sign of her being in cuffs recently.

"Ahh. That's better." She says, indicating the temperature of the water is to her liking.

She tilts her head back into the stream of the shower and starts rinsing her hair out. Just watching her enjoy the sensations of the water running over her body has my dick at attention. But if she's been in jail for as long as I've been in the hospital, we both need this shower. I reach over her and grab her shampoo.

Squeezing just a little into my palm, I work it into her hair while she continues to moan at the gentle pleasure.

She rinses her hair as I prepare to condition it. Just watching the water wash down over her breasts turns me on even more. It's been too long since I've been with her. I swear I'm going to explode the moment her lips wrap around me. I lather up her hair and then I use the soap and lather up her body. Going slowly and pinching the peaks of her breasts, letting her know my intentions for after this shower, or maybe in a few moments christening this shower.

My soapy hand goes down her flat stomach to her hips, soaping her as I go. My free hand wanders down the seam of her leg to where it joins to her honey pot. My thumb gently strokes on her clit as I put down the soap and rinse the excess soap off of my other hand.

I pull her body closer to mine and she leans into me. "Um. I've missed this." She purrs.

"Me too." I reply.

I slowly thrust two fingers inside her channel and damn, she's tighter than I remember. I've barely begun pleasuring her when I feel her body squeezing on my fingers. She's been depriving herself. I wait until the orgasm has passed before I shut off the water.

"Did they treat you okay at the jail?" I ask her.

"Yeah. I only had to stay in the jail a few hours and that was in an isolated cell." She explains.

"So, where have you been?"

"It was too risky to transport me to a safe house, so Viper and detective Ramirez decided it was best for me to stay in the officers' bunkroom. We had to make it look like I was in jail."

"So you had the deluxe accomodations of the jail." I joke with Joanie.

"Yeah, but I'm still trying to figure out how they knew I wasn't a real inmate, though the woman guard who registered me treated me as one."

"What did Ramirez say when he brought you in for booking?"

She shrugs and thinks back to the day of her booking. "Oh, he told the intake guard I was an IS-5." She finally says.

I chuckle. "The old IS-5."

Joanie nods in confusion. "Does it mean something?"

"Yup, I'll see you at five. It's a protective custody code. The officers came up with it for those entering protective custody or waiting until the heat dies down on a particular case if the person is at risk of being retaliated on." I explain the code. "The guards know it as an isolation code, so they put the inmate into an isolation cell, but when the computers pull the inmate lists for transportation to the jail or prison, they omit the IS-5's so they don't get transferred on accident. Then at shift change, a detective or someone else comes and orders the person's release as if they were just on a hold. The guards are none the wiser." I finish.

"That's neat. How they have a computer code that keeps those in protective custody out of the general population." Joanie says.

"Yeah, Hawk and Zeke programmed it a few years back when a CI accidentally got transferred to the general population in the big jail and the people he'd ratted on killed him." I admit to Joanie, so she understands why I was so worried about her being in jail.

"Well, Ramirez and the other detectives were nice, plus the girl named Beth Ann brought me some of my games so I could do something while I was stuck at police headquarters."

"That's good," I say as we move into the bedroom. "I've been bored out of my skull laying in that hospital bed. The television only had three channels that came in and for like three hours straight, each of them only broadcast soap operas. Then to top off everything, it was news for another four hours and not different news: **THE SAME FUCKING NEWS OVER AND OVER AGAIN.**" I say, emphasizing the last part so she knew just how bored I got.

"Oh, I'm so sorry." Joanie says.

"It's okay babe, it gave me plenty of time to think of all the ways I could make love to you. Where all I wanted to make love to you, and how I wanted to celebrate our love." I say as I place kisses on the nape of her neck.

She shivers at the touch of my lips on her skin. "What kinds of thoughts did you have?" She asks me.

"Oh, you're going to find out soon enough." I say, pushing her back onto the bed and continuing to kiss her neck and collarbone.

"Oh, really?" She questions, as my kisses trail further down and my lips land on her nipple.

I suckle it into my mouth giving it just a gentle tug between my teeth. Reminding her who is in charge here. She arches her back, enjoying the little pain I inflict on her nipple. I smile as I watch her reaction. Knowing my woman is going to want to rush this and I can't help it, I want to hurry up and bury myself inside of her too.

I continue my pursuit to her honey pot, making sure not to leave her breasts unattended for too long. Once my mouth leaves them, I replace the sensations on them with my hands gently fondling and every now and again pinching the pert tips. She smells so good. I love the way she smells. It's better in person than the aroma she leaves on the sheets. Over time, the aroma in our sheets fades. In person, it's strong all the time.

My mouth lands just above her mound and her legs open wider with anticipation of what I'm about to do. She knows me too well. We've only been sexually active before the incident for about a month, but we've kinda gotten into a routine. I don't know if it's all that blab on those talk shows I watched in the early mornings in the hospital or if it's just primal instinct, but I'm changing things up tonight.

I grab her hips and quickly flip her over and pull her to the edge of the bed. Her feet just touching the floor, putting her entrance in the perfect position for me. Her lips are glistening with wetness from her arousal as I position the tip of my cock there. I let out a low guttural moan, knowing this isn't going to be our normal gentle or slow love making session. I'm claiming her tonight. I've missed her and I need this hard and fast.

I still remember her issues and as I'm entering her channel, I whisper in her ear, "Let me know if this hurts you at all."

She nods as she moans while I'm entering. It's a pleasurable moan I've heard before and damn if I don't have to talk myself back from exploding the moment I feel the vibrations of her moan on my cock. If anything, it only fuels the fire inside of me.

I move slowly at first, allowing her to adjust the position if needed. Plus, it gives her body the opportunity to stretch out to my girth. She is the one that initiates the increased speed, and lord help me, I take her cue to heart. I'm slamming into her and she's moaning louder than I've heard her in the past. In octaves, I never knew she could hit.

"Yeah..." She pants out loudly "Ace... Oh God!"

All I can do is pound away and smile at the way she's moaning. Hell, she's past moaning, she's almost screaming.

That's when the door opens and I hear, "Oh shit, you're naked. Shit. Uh." It comes from a male voice I don't recognize.

"If the place ain't burning down get the fuck out and let me finish what I'm doing here!" I holler at the person that was intruding. Not missing a beat in my tapping Joanie's ass.

When we both come and I collapse on the bed. We're both covered in sweat from the intensity of the sex when I say, "I'm going to kill whoever that was just barging in like that." Having not recognized the voice.

Joanie blushes, and it's apparent she recognized the voice. She giggles and says, "That was my uncle Hunter. Which means Skye and Mikal might be here too. We were probably disturbing someone's sleep." She chuckles, but I can tell she's a bit embarrassed about being caught making love.

"Babe, he only saw my naked ass." I say to ease her embarrassment. "Anyway, he shouldn't have barged into the room if he didn't want to see a man screwing his woman."

"But I've known Hunter and Skye since I was a baby, and it's just..."

"Awkward?" I supply.

She nods.

"Jo, they're going to have to learn that you're a grown woman who has sex with me. You're not the little girl they raised anymore. Your dad is always going to see you as his little girl, and I get that, but he's accepted the fact I want to be with you in every way a man wants to be with a woman. Now his teammates will have to accept it too."

She smiles and I can't help but place a kiss on those beautiful lips. I wait until she dozes off before I get up. I pull on a pair of sweatpants and a tank top before I head over to the next door. Joanie's old room is apparently being occupied by Ghost's teammate Hunter.

I knock on the door and wait for him to answer. Instead of him answering, a woman answers the door. She's got to be in her forties and looks exhausted. Fuck. They must have driven in today, and I just woke her up.

"Hi," she whispers out.

"Hi," I say back. "Um, is Hunter here?"

She smiles at me and says, "He went for a run. He was mumbling something about seeing things he shouldn't be seeing at his age."

I can't help the chuckle that slips out. "Yeah, I'm sorry if we were keeping you awake. I didn't know Viper had put anyone in the room next to me. I just got out of the hospital and my girl surprised me."

"Uh, huh. We kinda heard her screaming and thought you might be hurting her." She informs me of what made Hunter barge in.

I must be blushing pretty hard because she lets out a low chuckle and says, "Hell, Hunter delivered Joanie, so I'm not really sure why seeing you and your girl having sex could have upset him. Unless you were having sex with Jo..." She trails off and I feel Joanie walking up behind me.

"Hi Skye," Joanie says meekly.

"Hi." Skye crosses her arms and her demeanor towards me now changes. She's shooting daggers at me. It's apparent no one has told them about our relationship status.

I pull Joanie in close to me. I'm not shy. The entire N.R.T. team knows about our relationship. Ghost gave us permission to date, and little does anyone know I'm going to pop the question soon. Before Skye can ask any questions of Joanie and me, we hear footsteps approaching behind us.

Hunter passes by Joanie and only shakes his head at the two of us and just says, "I hope you two can face the consequences of your actions. Sneaking around when her father isn't here. What do you think I'm going to do, keep your dirty little secret?"

He looks at me and says, "You should know the rules." He pokes at my chest and that's when I snap.

I grab the finger he's jabbing in my chest and twist his arm around behind his back in one swift move. Pulling him around so his back is to my chest. He's the same height as me, but I've got more muscle mass. I can even feel the finger popping in my grip. I've probably already broken it.

I lean in close to his ear and say in a low voice, "Motherfucker, I know the rules. I followed the rules to a fucking T. I just got out of the fucking hospital after protecting Jo from an attack. We've been separated for over two weeks because of the shit that went down. Ghost fucking gave us permission to date. Joanie is a grown ass woman and she can choose if she wants to make love to me or if we go at it hard and fast. I'm tired of you guys all treating her like she's some fuck up."

That's when I feel the zing. It's not from Hunter. No, it's his fucking wife. She apparently still suffers from some PTSD from something that happened years ago. I look down and sticking out of my bicep is a fucking switchblade. She buried the damn knife all the way to the base.

"Fuckin bitch!" I say. I'm not a man to hit a woman, but calling her names I'll do.

"Don't call my wife that!" Hunter exclaims as he tries to lunge towards me, since I let him go at the searing pain in my bicep.

I continue to fight him. He's holding his arm close to him indicating I've broken his finger and maybe his wrist. I'm down to one good arm since his wife stuck a blade in my bicep. He's protecting his woman, and I'm protecting mine. After a few more swings at each other we hear, "My own men are fighting?"

Viper's voice booms through the common room. He's pissed and we can all tell it. Both Hunter and I quit fighting and look down to where he is standing with the rest of the men from the mission, including Ghost.

"And what might I ask are you two fighting about?" He asks.

"Just a mere misunderstanding about our relationship." Joanie answers Viper's question for us.

Viper chuckles and nods at what she's said. "Ah, so the uncle is protecting his niece and the boyfriend protecting his girlfriend. We don't need soap operas, we've got enough drama here under our own roof."

I see Hunter pale when Ghost doesn't flinch at hearing Joanie is dating me, and the fact Viper felt comfortable enough to say it out in the open. It meant a lot.

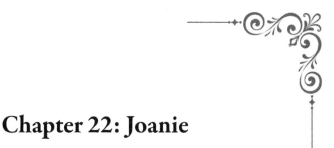

Chapter 22: Joanie

After Viper settled Hunter's and Ace's disagreement about my status. The two men finally shake hands like they're told to do. Ghost takes Hunter to the hospital after Ace gave his finger and wrist a once over and suggested it best.

Viper and Ghost both looked at the knife sticking out of Ace's wound and offered to take him to the hospital, too. But Ace being Ace told them he didn't want to go for reasons. His reasons being he didn't want to get into another fight with Hunter, and he didn't do well with doctors poking and prodding on him again so soon after his release.

Instead, I get the honor of helping to remove Skye's switchblade from his bicep and stitching up the gaping wound it left. I had figured that seeing the hole in his arm and the blood, I'd gag. I listen as Ace instructs me on how to sew up the muscle tissue and then the outer layers of skin.

Once I'm done stitching his bicep up, he looks over the wound and at my stitching job. Ace says, "Nice work for your first time."

"Thanks." I say, feeling the heat rising in my cheeks.

I still can't believe that my boyfriend and my uncle got into a fight over me having sex. Heck, Ace was certain that Hunter hadn't seen me, but lo-and-behold he'd gotten an eye full of my naked body. Not that I'm shy about my body, but I've grown up with Hunter and the rest of dad's SEAL team. They've watched me grow up and now he's seen me naked. It was cool as a child, but after puberty I kinda didn't want any of dad's men seeing me naked.

"Oh, these came for you while we were locked up." Ace hands me some mail.

I look through the mail and it's a letter from Jen. She got the address from Liam. It's short and she wants to make sure I'm okay and it's cool to mail me letters while she's in boot camp. I feel Ace moving behind me. He's holding me, concerned about me. I'm not sure if I can take Jen's excitement about the Navy when I'm still hurt by what they did to me. Letting me get all the way to MEPS and through the testing done there, only to be denied at the last minute. It still hurts. I had been honest about everything, and they hadn't.

Ace's arms wrap around my waist and I feel the gentle kisses on the back of my neck. I don't think he's reading her letter over my shoulder, but it wouldn't matter to me, as we have no secrets. He keeps kissing my neck as I open the second letter. It's from the college I applied to at the end of my school year.

"I got accepted." I almost shout.

I feel Ace's lips curve as he places another kiss on the back of my neck. My eyes continue to scan the letter. It states that since I was so late in applying for the fall semester and my high school diploma is from a home schooling out of state, I'm required to attend a college placement testing before I can schedule classes. My eyes land on the end of the letter, and it says I have to call the school to schedule a placement test and a campus tour before the end of the month, or else I will forfeit my spot.

"I'll call Monday and schedule the testing." I mumble to myself, as Ace is in the mood to celebrate again.

Even with fresh stitches in his arm, he's already wanting to take a turn in the sheets again. I make a mental note to keep the moaning down so not to disturb our new neighbors. This would be so much better if we had a place of our own.

I feel Ace's hand slide between my legs as he positions me on my side and his thumb strums on my clit. Immediately taken over by arousal, I drop the letters beside the bed. My hand reaches back and I grab his hip, letting him know I want him. He responds by spreading my lips open and sliding in gently.

As he begins to move inside me, I can't help the goosebumps that rise on my body. Everywhere he touches me leaves a trail of goosebumps. We make love coming together for the second time tonight. Finally, falling asleep with him still buried deep inside me.

Just like most nights when I wake the next morning, neither of us has moved. What wakes me is Ace's cock hardening against my thigh. I slide out of his arms and he rolls over onto his back. He's still asleep when I kiss his exposed nipple. He moans the moment my lips leave his nipple.

I look up to see his eyes fluttering open, still sleepy. I trail kisses down his ripped abs. He's already hard by the time I get down to my giggle stick as he loves to refer to his cock as. I run my tongue around the purplish mushroom shaped head of his cock, causing him to stir awake even more.

"Babe, you know how to drive me crazy." He moans out as I wrap my lips around the head and take him into my mouth.

I continue to suck and lick on his shaft, pausing momentarily before I move down and give his balls each a gentle suck into my mouth. Ace lets out a pleasurable moan as I release his nut with a loud pop. I trail my tongue up the vein on the underside of his dick all the way up to the tip. Swirling my tongue around the tip before I take him into my mouth once again.

Ace's fingers find my scalp and he gently tugs on my hair as he approaches his orgasm. I enjoy the feeling of him pulling on my hair, knowing he's enjoying the pleasure I'm giving him. I start tasting the tang of his orgasm as he's building. It feels like his cock expands in my mouth just before he explodes, shooting jets of come into my mouth.

I wait until his cock stops twitching and I've swallowed all of his come before I slide my mouth back up to the tip and allow him to pop out. He dribbles some come on my lip as I'm licking up and down his shaft one last time before I climb up and give him a good morning kiss. I lick the come off my lips, enjoying the taste of his essence.

We make love the rest of the morning until we have to emerge from our room for something to eat. When we do, everyone is sitting around the dining room table where Annie, Skye and Cynthia have prepared breakfast for everyone. Just as tradition back home. This place is feeling more like home every day.

I notice Hunter has a cast on his arm and I walk over to where he's standing near the breakfast spread. "What did the doctor say?" I ask.

"Broken wrist, broken pointer finger, and given the advice of I'm getting too old to pick fights with younger men." He chuckles as he says that last bit.

"I'm sorry Uncle Hunter. I didn't know you were coming in." I'm about to explain about being in the police custody for the last two weeks when he interrupts me.

"It's okay, Viper explained to me while we were waiting to be seen by the doctor. I'm sorry I didn't realize you and Ace were dating with your father's approval. I'm so used to the rebellious Joanie. I don't know this new settled down little lady."

We sit at the table. Skye, me, Hunter and Ace all sit near each other. I notice Mikal is missing from the breakfast gathering, and Skye quickly tells me he's still sleeping. I'm curious where he's sleeping at since she and Hunter have my old room and it's the only one I knew was open. That's when I'm informed with my dad going crazy while I was in 'jail' and Ace in the hospital. Their house got completed and the team has moved on to working on Viper and Cynthia's house. So, Mikal is staying in my mom's old room.

While everyone is still at breakfast, I figure it's the perfect time to let them all know about me being accepted to the community college for the fall semester. It goes over better than anything else I've ever told my family about doing. Of course, there are the typical questions of what I'm planning on studying and when I mention something in the medical field, I see Hunter puff his chest out. Everyone that knows me well is congratulating me. Even my parents. The one question that looms over me that Viper asked is, "Are you going to attend virtual classes or in person?"

I'm unsure why he's asked, but I shrug and say, "I'm considering a mixture of both. Since I've been homeschooled all my life, I'm not sure about going full on in person classes."

He only nods at my response and then turns and whispers something to Hawk. Who in return excuses himself and heads into the security room.

I knew some of the paramedic/EMT classes had to be done in person as they are hands on, but other classes I can opt for online and even continue to help at the building sites around my class schedule.

The next hour or so is spent with Hunter, my dad and Viper questioning me about my plans on getting to the college and my scheduling of classes. I explain to the three of them and Ace that I have to first attend the orientation and college placement testing before I can schedule my classes. As for getting to and from classes, I'm a bit reliant on the men of N.R.T. since I don't have a mode of transportation.

Hawk comes out of the security room and whispers something to Viper. He nods in response to whatever Hawk said. Hawk turns and heads back into the security room. A few minutes later, Hawk returns and hands something to Ace, who nods at him as I'm continued to be drilled. He opens a piece of paper up and reads from it. "So school starts in the middle of August. It's the middle of July. That gives us a month to get your school schedule." He says.

I notice the men all glancing at their phones within moments of Hawk leaving. They only acknowledge something and then place their phones back wherever they keep them. With the end of the questioning, ending with Viper, Ace and my dad all deciding that after my college placement testing and eventual scheduling, they'll decide then about manpower and transportation for me. I'll keep them informed of when the placement and orientation are scheduled for when I schedule it on Monday. Overall, I'm excited since everyone is backing me going to college.

Just as I'm about to get up from the breakfast table, Ace stops me. He says, "You're my woman, and we don't want you going anywhere without the ability to contact us."

He nods at Viper, who slides a cellphone down the table to me. It's been almost six months since I had a phone. I almost don't know who to thank first.

"Now don't go giving out that number. It's for emergencies only. We've uploaded all the N.R.T. members' numbers into the phone. If you call one of us, we will answer if we aren't on a mission." Viper says as I pick up the phone from the table.

"Thank you." I say meekly.

"Now I would say no social media or gaming apps, but that will be between you and Ace. However, there will be absolutely no photos taken inside the areas of headquarters that are currently off-limits to you," Viper says, informing me of the rules about cameras in the other areas of headquarters.

I nod in understanding. Picking up the phone, I head into the common room. There are so many things I feel like I've missed out on over the last few months. As I sit down on one of the sofa's I start by setting up my background and lock screens with some of my favorite things. Since I haven't got photos of me and Ace yet, I'll have to go with the generic pre-loaded backgrounds and themes I find on the phone manufacturers' shop.

I can hear Ace and the others talking in the other room, and it fills me with joy. We don't have to be attached at the hip all the time, but just knowing he is nearby is enough. As I flip through the backgrounds and themes, I realize how having a generic one is better than putting one of Ace and myself on it. I had always wondered why my mom never put photos of me, Liam or herself and dad on her phone, but I'm realizing it's a safety measure.

Monday I called and scheduled for my college placement testing and for a tour of the campus. I've been behind the eight ball, as my dad would phrase it on everything. The lady I spoke with at the school told me I was lucky, all but the last group of orientation and testing were full. She scheduled me for it and informed me the orientation and testing was on Friday of the next week. I have to be there at eight am for testing which she says will take until noon, and then the orientation starts at two and lasts until four, ending with a tour of the campus and going over the results of my tests and scheduling my classes.

I relay all the information to Ace and Viper. Viper isn't happy that it's an all-day affair. Although it gives Ace and me time to have lunch together and just get away like we had planned to a few weeks ago. Viper approves Ace to go with me and orders him not to leave my side unless they won't let him into the testing area. They are still taking my protection seriously and I don't know why. Didn't they catch the people who attacked me and Ace? I know I've proven that I'm not going to run away, heck I'm dating Ace, and I really love him. I don't see my life without him in it.

The morning of my testing comes and I can't believe how nervous I am about the whole starting college and touring the campus. I've gone through four outfits before I settle on a black pair of jeans and a vee neck light green tee shirt that doesn't hug my body too tight. Thanks to my dad moving in I've got more of a selection of clothes since he brought our house belongings with him a few weeks ago.

Ace has been such a sport watching me change outfits this morning while he's grabbed a pair of his black tactical pants and a black polo shirt. When I'm finally ready, we head out to the campus where my testing is taking place. The school had mailed me a confirmation letter with a map of the campus so I'd know where we could park and where I was to check in for my test at.

I'm nervous the whole ride to the campus, but Ace tries to calm me down by telling me how smart I am and how much he and my parents believe in me. Even though he's trying to calm me down I'm nervous as hell.

Chapter 23: Ace

Jo is nervous about testing this morning. She's dressed and redressed until I tell her she had to choose an outfit so we could go. She looks so deliciously sexy in the jeans and tee shirt she finally decided on. I tried to settle her nerves by telling her how proud I am of her and that she's a very smart woman, but I don't think she believes me. So, I make a crack that she has to be smart, she asks me why and I replied with "because you picked me." That prompted her to give me a smart elbow to the ribs and we both laugh. It had the desired effect, she relaxed.

We pull into the parking lot of the main building and head inside. There are summer classes going on so a few students mill about in the hallways. I couldn't bring my sidearm with me as the college has a no gun policy. They don't care if you have an open carry permit or not. I could normally have brought my sidearm if I'd been here on business, but since I'm with a student and not here on business, I didn't want to cause any waves, so I left it back at headquarters.

Jo checks in with the counselor's office and they show her back to an area where she will take a computerized test. The lady that checks her in tells me I can come back at noon or if I choose, I can wait on the benches just outside the counselor offices. I opt for the latter and watch as more kids her age file into the office area. Some parents drop them off and leave, promising to pick them up at noon, or when the child calls them to let them know they have finished testing, or rejoin them for the tour of the school. Only a few of the parents or significant others stay around to hang out while their loved ones take the computerized test.

I'm a people person. More of a people watcher. I pretend to be occupied in my phone, but really I'm observing what's going on around me. I see several students going back and forth to their classes. Nothing suspicious. I even watch the security guard and that is where the suspicious activity is happening. Not really suspicious, just unsettling to me.

There is only one security guard in the office, and I notice he doesn't have a sidearm or even handcuffs. Periodically he leaves and gets into a golf cart, riding around and checking on the other buildings on campus. During this time, his office is left with no one to watch the security of the main building. To me, it's a red flag. I watch as several students go into the office looking for the officer, not finding him and leave several minutes later. A few hang out in the office and wait for him to come back and help them with whatever they need.

All kinds of security issues are going through my head. If someone really wanted to put a hurt on the school, they could come into the security office, hack into his computer and access the student id cards, parking passes, and other simple things. But they could even hack into the phone system from there and shut out everyone from being able to call out for help. I'm not liking what I'm seeing.

Joanie comes out of the testing area around eleven and she's allowed to leave the campus until one thirty, when we have to meet back at the testing area for a check in and then the campus tour begins. For the tour, she's allowed to have at least two companions with her. The lady called them companions, but she hinted at parents. She's trying to be politically correct and not offend anyone.

I take her hand and we head out to my truck and I drive her to a close by restaurant. The whole time I listen as she tells me about the tests she took and how she was overly worried, but it was really easy. She even was one of the first to finish and since they did the tests at their own pace, she finished all of them fairly early.

After lunch, we head back to the campus for the college tour. I'm not overly thrilled, but Joanie is. It's the first time in her life she'll be attending classes outside of her home. Once everyone is accounted for, they split the group into smaller groups to allow for the guides to be heard and to answer questions.

Our tour begins right where we stand in the main hall. We get a quick tour of the main areas students use, the security office, the bookstore, the counselor's offices, and the financial aid office before we head out into the quad. The quad has several pathways and several places where students can sit and study or eat. Each pathway leads to another building. The way the college has set up the different buildings according to their different majors. There is an English building, a science building, a liberal arts building, and even a building for those majoring in physical education.

Since summer classes are going on we don't go into the buildings themselves. Most of the buildings are the same anyway with classrooms except for the science and physical education buildings. Here we get to see the labs for the different science majors. Such as the nursing hands-on labs, and the indoor swimming pool in the physical education building. We get to see the campus library and the campus cafeteria.

I get the feeling these tour guides are more about selling the students on coming to their college over actually getting quality students to attend. I'm looking around our group of prospective students and their parents or significant others. Most of them are young, like Joanie, having just finished high school and looking for the next step in their lives. But what strikes me as odd is these kids come from all kinds of backgrounds. Some of them you can tell come from really poor backgrounds, while others are from more affluent backgrounds. The whole time we are touring, the guide is talking about how the school will help with all the financial aid needs that a student may have. It makes me wonder why the affluent kids aren't looking into the four-year universities.

As we walk up a hill heading towards the campus housing, which strikes me as kind of odd for a community college. The parking lot in front of the housing area is near empty, and the guide is going on about the housing units and how they're split up not to be like your typical campus dorms. They're more like apartments with three to four students per unit, but each student has their own room. The students share a bathroom or two, depending on the number of students in the unit. She continues to describe the living room as a common area the students get to decorate as a group and the kitchenette as a place where the students can grab a quick meal or snack before attending classes or after the cafeteria has closed down.

She reaches into her pocket and grabs out a key to the unit she's going to show us. As the door opens, she lets our tour group in before she steps into the entranceway. That's when I hear the tour guide squeal. Behind her are two men with purple and white bandanas covering their faces. One man has a knife sticking into the tour guide's side as he roughly pushes her into the apartment, and they close and lock the door behind them.

The second man orders the men into what would be the common room of the little housing unit and the rest of the women into the kitchenette. I can only comply as my side arm is at headquarters, and I don't want to upset the hostage takers until I can fully assess the situation.

Our group was made up of four prospective students. Joanie, another girl about her age, a teenage boy and a man who looked to be in his late twenties. The other girl had brought her parents with her to tour the campus, while the teenage boy had only brought his mom. The older man was alone, making our group have five women and four men. Easy enough to be over taken by just two terrorists. They might be just gang bangers, but in my book they were terrorists.

I had seen my fair share of terrorist hostage situations in my years as a SEAL. I knew the best thing for us to do was cooperate with them to keep them calm and from hurting us. Everyone was panicking, which was normal in the situation. It bought me time to grab my cell phone and hit my speed dial for headquarters. I left the speaker off so no one would hear my call since I kept my phone in my pocket.

I knew when Zeke or Hawk answered and heard the chaos, they would alert the officials. Viper knew where I was at and with the caller ID at headquarters the guys would know it was me calling and could track my location down to a pinpoint on the map.

"Everyone put your phones in the bucket, my brother here is passing around along with your wallets or purses." The man with a knife to our tour guide's side says.

His buddy comes around and collects all our cellphones, wallets, and purses. No one notices my phone is actively in a call. All I can hope for is that it stays that way. I can't pass an assessment on to my guys, but at least they know I need help. Next, he ties our hands behind our backs and our legs together at the ankles, forcing us to sit up against a wall. They tie the women's hands behind their backs and lead them into one bedroom.

As hostages, we can't talk about escape or overthrowing the two men since the one that tied us up is standing guard over us. I'm worried about what is happening to my Joanie, as well as the other women. That's when the other men and I hear the scream come from down the hall.

The other man about my age struggles against his restraints and our captor pulls a gun out of the waistband of his pants and says, "Nu uh, I wouldn't do that if I were you."

Thankfully my friend is smart and sits back down having seen the gun. We continue to hear the women screaming. The sounds of their screams are muffled, not just by the closed door, but it sounds as if they've gagged them. I can hear the fear in their muffled screams.

A knock comes to the door and our captor answers it. In walk several more of the purple and white bandana terrorists. One of them heads straight down the hall to where the women are at. He's having a heated argument with the one that's in the room with the women. This isn't good. There's a riff in their system which means one of them could go bat shit crazy and kill us all. All I can do right now is hope that the guys have figured out we seriously need thier help.

Chapter 24: Joanie

Everything happened so fast. One minute I was enjoying walking the campus with Ace and the next I'm living my worse nightmare. I knew I didn't need a house on campus, but it was part of the tour before I could see my counselor to schedule my classes.

When I'd heard the girl giving us a tour scream, my heart dropped into my stomach. The fear from just a few weeks ago crept back in. This couldn't be happening again.

The women have been separated from the men and they have taken us down the hallway into a bedroom. When the door to the bedroom closes, he ties our ankles and gags us with rags. I can tell this has been planned. Everything these two idiots need is already here. They're not improvising restraints or gags, they're here already.

I'm looking around to see if there's a way out of this apartment. It was a ground floor unit, and probably the one they used just for showing. It's not got furnishings, but there are some curtains and window shades on the windows. The room we're being held in is facing the main campus and has a window. It's small and most of us women could fit through the window if needed as an escape.

I hear one of the older women scream even through her gag, it's enough to pull me from my assessment of the room. When I look over, our captor has taken his knife and cut her shirt open from collar to hem. He's taking his knife and cutting the arms off the shirt. The sicko is laughing at the terror he's instilling in the woman.

I see tears flowing down her face as she shakes her head. The shirt drops to the floor in pieces. He does the same to the skirt she's wearing, cutting it off her body. He follows suit with each girl in line. I can't help it. When he gets to me, I cry too. Even though I thought I was tougher than that. The tip of the knife blade cuts me in a few places on my legs. Since I was the only one to wear jeans today, it's harder for him to cut. Just knowing how close the knife is and that one slip might cut an artery and end my life, the tears flow.

I wish now I'd told Ace how much I love him, because I'm sure I won't get to see him again. My heart hurts and the tears flow harder as I think of all the things I haven't said to my parents or Ace. I think about the things I would do differently and how I would treat my parents better.

"Mmm. You ladies look delicious." Our captor says.

We're all sitting there in nothing but our underwear and bras. The two older women aren't ashamed of their bodies and sit up straight against the wall. While myself and the other two younger girls feel his eyes on us and pull our knees close to our chests to hide ourselves from him as much as possible.

He grabs the tour guide and pulls her up roughly by her arm. He pulls the gag out of her mouth and sticks a finger into her mouth as she continues to cry. He's making this sexual, at least for him. I can see the hard-on through his pants. He's not being shy about being aroused by all of us being scared by what he might do to us.

The man cuts her bra open and he leers over her body. We can hear her begging him not to do what he's doing to her, but it only seems to egg him on even more. He spins her around and forces her face against the wall, using his knife to cut away her underwear. The rest of us women all know what he's about to do to her and we are unable to help her out. All we can do is sit and watch, or give her some respect and turn our heads. The older two ladies turn their heads to show her some privacy since they know she's about to be raped and they want to give her the respect of not watching the man take her against her will.

She's still babbling her protests and it's gotten under his skin, some it seems. As he reaches up and replaces the gag in her mouth. It only muffles her cries of protests. He frees himself from his pants and proceeds to take her. It's a violent mess. There is blood running down her leg and when he's finished with her, he pulls out and drops her to the floor.

He grabs me next. Fear courses through me as I've seen how he took our tour guide. I've had problems in the past with mentally shutting out people and sex not being enjoyable. I feel the tip of the knife cut my bra and I mentally prepare myself for what is about to happen. I can't help the tears, but I don't beg him not to do this, it only seemed to make him happier that she didn't want it to happen.

My bra slips down my arms to where they are tied behind my back as my breasts hang free. He roughly fondles one of my breasts and weirdly I now notice how sensitive they are.

"Oh, I bet the guys love your tits. They're the right size. What are you, a C cup or a D?" He asks me as he continues to fondle my breasts.

I can't answer with the gag in my mouth. But I don't think he was really wanting an answer. He spins me around to face the wall and takes the knife to my underwear in the same way he'd done our tour guide. I can see her still laying on the floor crying. I don't blame her. He took something from her she didn't want to give him.

Just as I feel the tip of his cock at my entrance, I hear the bedroom door open and another man's voice say, "What the fuck, dude?"

"I'm just getting some good use of the female hostages. You know what they're doing to our guys in jail."

"You know the cops won't negotiate if they're hurt. They're just pawns to get our higher ups out of jail so we can make necessary trades." The second guy argues.

"I'm just tasting the product. Don't worry, bro. The cops will give us anything we want to get these people back alive. Nothing says we can't sample the goods. Hell, look at this one's tits. She'd make a good one for the clubhouse."

He spins me around. I'm completely naked. The other man's eyes peruse over my body. He licks his lips and I know he's mentally fucking me. I've seen that same look from a few of the guys at N.R.T. before Ace and I started dating.

"You can enjoy that later. Right now, we have a call to make with our demands."

"All right." My captor says as I hear him zipping up the fly of his pants.

I can't believe how close I was to being raped. The two of them head out, leaving another man watching over us. This man only looks barely old enough to shave. I don't feel as threatened by this man as I did with the other one. Even though he's holding a pistol on us. He's just as mean as the others, but I don't feel like he's going to rape me. He's even trying to avert his eyes away from us as long as we stay sitting where we are.

Chapter 25: Viper

"Yo, Viper, we got a situation!" Hawk calls sticking his head out of the security room.

I get up from my desk where I had been sitting down going over the monthly finances. I hate this part of owning a business. Separating business expenses from personal expenses and recording them. It gives me a headache for at least three days, and let's not talk about tax season, that's a month long migraine of write-offs and deprecation.

"I so need to hire an accountant." I mutter as I stand up and make my way to the security office. "What's up?" I ask, closing the door behind me.

"Well, we got a weird call from Ace." Hawk states, cutting to the point.

"You sure he didn't ass dial us while they were taking a tour of the campus?" I ask, looking at my watch and knowing the itinerary.

"That's what we thought at first. But the voices are more muffled and none of them sound like someone giving a tour." He paused and I could see the concern in his eyes. "Then we heard the muffled screams."

"Fuck." I say, running my hand through my hair. "Zeke, get me a location on that call."

"Already on it." Zeke replies. "They're in the campus housing. I can't tell exactly what unit, but I can tell you the address."

I grab out my phone and dial up detective Ramirez. We'd left Ace and Joanie out of the loop on some of the information about the gang members we'd caught when we did our sting operation with the gang unit. I even went to their bail hearing. The judge had given them no bond with their links to outside countries. Their brothers that were there had made statements about getting them out. At the time, I wasn't sure what it would be, but I had put all the men from the mission on alert for some kind of crazy attack on the jail and prison system. But nothing had happened. **Until now.**

I filled detective Ramirez in on what I knew was going on and he filled me in on the call the police had received about having nine hostages. The hostage takers wanted their people released in exchange for the hostages they held.

"What are your people doing?"

"SWAT is currently discussing strategy with the Chief of police. They won't even leave for the college for close to an hour." Ramirez tells me.

"My guys and I have a pin-pointed location and can be there in thirty. If you can get your officers to the school and lock down the main campus buildings, and evacuate as many as possible from the surrounding housing units without raising suspicion, it would be a great help."

"Roger, I'll tell the SWAT team you guys are there, so they won't shoot friendlies when they get there. Anything else I can do?"

"Nope."

"Alright, be safe, friend."

I look at Hawk and Zeke and say, "Alpha team meets in the tact room, on the double. Get Hunter down there, since my medic is a hostage." I say as I turn and head toward the door. "And whatever you do, don't let Ghost in this room!"

"Yes, sir." The two men say in unison.

They send out the message and within a few minutes, my team is assembled in the tact room. I'm passing out weapons, vests, and tact helmets. No one asks a question. They take what I give to them and head over to grab ammo and other needed items before getting into our black tactical van. On the outside, it looks like a normal van, but inside, we've made it into a van that can transport nine men and has a communication station.

We get into the van and Razor asks, "Where to?"

"The community college."

"Fuck," is the unanimous response of the guys as Razor turns and heads the van out of our garage.

As he drives, I give my guys the brief of the hostage situation. We don't know the number of hostage takers, but we know they've got nine hostages. Also, we know they're being held in the residential units. We go over the plans to minimize any injury to those not involved.

"Taze, I want you on the sniper rifle. Ready to take anyone out that tries to exit or harm the hostages."

"Roger that."

"Hunter, I want you at the back of the breach team. I don't want you getting hurt since you're my only medic, and you only have one good hand. But I want you to provide any medical attention once we secure the hostages."

"Got it." I can tell he's wondering if this is the college his niece was touring and if she's a hostage.

"Yes, but I don't know." I say out loud to him. "Will you be okay if she is?" I'm not totally lying to him, but I know Ace is a hostage and if he followed my orders, then it's highly likely Joanie is, too. But if I give him too much information, he'll be no good to the rest of the team.

"I'll be fine. If they've hurt her, I'll kill them for Ghost."

We pull up in the parking lot of the campus and can already see the officers that responded to the college in order to protect the students have locked the main campus down and are evacuating the surrounding resident, housings. They can't evacuate the location where the hostages are since it'll tip off the terrorists we are about to come in. Hawk is giving directions to Razor about where we are in relation to Ace's phone location.

Razor parks our van in a community parking lot. He's not too close to the buildings so not to give us away. "The building on the left is where Ace's signal is coming from." He says, taking off his seatbelt and climbing into the back area to grab his weapon.

It's a three story building with four units per level. Meaning we have twelve potential places for the hostages to be held. A few minutes later, we see a student exit one of the upper level apartments and start down the stairs. We inform Hawk so he can listen for the student to pass by the apartment where Ace's phone is located. This could eliminate half of the apartments since there are two sets of stairs, one going to the apartments on the North side and the other going to the apartments on the South side. Just as we are about to give up, Hawk hears the student outside the apartment. We now know they're in one of the two downstairs apartments on the North side since that was the side the student was using.

Taze hops out of our van and finds a good spot for cover and where he can see both the lower apartments. Once he's in place, he checks in as he looks through his high power scope and starts analyzing the two apartments.

"They've split up the hostages." Taze's voice says in my earpiece. "They're all in the left apartment. Men are being held in the common room. I count four of them."

I can tell he's scanning the apartment, looking for the rest of the hostages. Taze is too quiet for too long and I can feel the tension rising in me.

He finally comes back over my earpiece. "Women are in the back bedroom. Whatever you do, don't send Hunter into that room without first removing the terrorists." He says telling me everything I need to know.

His few words tell me he's seen something and he knows Hunter won't like it.

"I see only four guards, two with the men, one with the women, and the fourth is roving."

"Roger that. If the guard watching Joanie hurts her, or makes a move to hurt her, take him out."

"Roger."

We form up and quickly but quietly make our way over to the breezeway between the two apartments. I take the lead, not my normal, but my friend and my mentor's daughter are both being held in there. I reach over and give a rap on the door and then go back to the side. Where we are positioned means the person answering has to step out the door where we can neutralize them.

Just like the rulebook, someone answers the door and, not seeing anyone, steps out into the doorway. I reach out my arm and grab the kid by the collar, throwing him off balance. As I'm throwing him to the ground and disarming him the rest of the team heads inside. As I'm placing the zip tie cuffs on the first terrorists, I hear a scuffle and some hella noise from inside. I pick up my terrorist up and take him inside so I can watch him and help to free up the hostages.

When I walk into the apartment, the sight before me makes me die laughing. Razor had been the first through the open door and had managed to sneak up behind the roving guard. Apparently, in the scuffle to subdue him Razor's prosthetic had come loose. The poor kid is thrashing around screaming, "I've pulled his arm off! Oh, my God, I've pulled a person's arm off!"

Hunter the last man to enter, is dying laughing and so is Ace, who is still restrained against a wall. It confused the other hostages, what is so funny. The whole time, Razor is still trying to subdue the suspect and his prosthetic arm is flailing around, not doing what he wants it to do.

"Shut the fuck up, man, and get the fuck down." Razor says, the frustration coming through in his voice.

Thankfully the suspect obeys his commands and gets down putting his gun on the ground in front of him. He's too freaked out about pulling off Razor's arm not to comply. Razor places a knee on his back and one handedly applies the zip tie cuffs to the suspect. Helping him up to his feet, he walks him over to where we've placed his friend.

I'm broken from my chuckling when I hear my men call for me from down the hall. Both Razor and I double time it down the small hallway. Opening the door, we can't believe what we're seeing. Our teammates have subdued the other two terrorists. But the sight in that room is horrific.

"Get Hunter in here. STAT." I say to no one in particular.

I can tell my men have grabbed the terrorists and are taking them back to the holding area and getting Hunter. Razor and I are blocking his view of Joanie. We need him to treat the lady laying on the floor. She's bleeding from her privates and her breathing is slowing. She needs medical attention immediately. Hunter doesn't need to see the state of undress Joanie is in at the moment.

With only a nod of my head to the injured woman, he immediately goes to her and renders her the aid he can. Taze has made it into the apartment during the chaos and approaches me.

"Do you want me to get Ace out of here before the paramedics come back here for the women?" He asks me.

"No. He won't leave. He'll want to be with Joanie." I know Ace too well.

Before long, the paramedics and swat are milling around the little apartment. They have their questions that need answering, but all five of the women need to see a doctor, and I make sure the officers know it. With them all in varying states of undress, I know they need to be seen for mental trauma.

While the paramedics get the first girl onto a gurney and prepared to roll out to their ambulance, I turn to Joanie and ask, "Did they rape you?"

She's naked and shivering. I want to give her clothing, but I know if they raped her, the cops will need the evidence from her body, so I can't offer her anything for protection at the moment.

"No. Almost, but then t-they came back and did it to her again." She says shakily.

Deep inside, I'm thankful they didn't rape her, but I'm also angry that we didn't get here in time to protect the other woman from the abuse she endured. I nod at her statement to me and allow Ace to take my place by Joanie's side until the paramedics come back. I head over to inform the lead SWAT officer about Joanie's admittance to what happened to the one woman.

Chapter 26: Joanie

After the men left for their phone call, I tried to help our tour guide. She just flinched at any touch I gave her. My hands still tied behind my back, all I could do really was kneel down and rub on her back to let her know she wasn't alone. I could feel her body shake as she continued to cry. The young kid they'd left to supervise us didn't seem to care about what I was doing. As long as we didn't attempt an escape, he seemed okay.

When his buddies came back, they dismissed him back to where he had originally been. The man that had been about to rape me grabbed me up and threw me over to where the other women were sitting. I felt my head hit the wall and before long a trickle of blood could be felt going down my forehead.

His buddy grabbed up our tour guide and they both took her at the same time. We couldn't do anything but watch. These two jerks were taking her, hurting her, and all we could do was watch and scream out against our gags. When they were done with her, they grabbed me up again.

The one with the knife was using the tip to go down my body. Just as he's getting to my belly button, there's a commotion in the hallway.

"What now? Can't that little fucker control four restrained men?" His friend asks, as he heads over to the door.

I can hear someone screaming frantically about pulling someone's arm off. That's when I realize it's got to be Razor struggling with one of the hostage takers. I know we are about to be rescued so I can take anything this guy dishes out before they rescue us.

"Fuck." The guy at the door mutters right as the door opens and slams him in the face.

The guy in front of me turns around to see two of the biggest, burliest men of N.R.T. with their sights on him. He immediately drops his knife and puts his hands in the air. I wish my legs weren't bound or else I would kick him in the nuts for everything he's done to the other women and myself.

Grainger lowers his rifle and removes the man from in front of me. The moment he sees my state of undress, he says, "Fuck, Ace is going to fuck these guys up." He immediately turns around, giving me some privacy. Wolf takes the man from his custody and quickly attaches zip tie cuffs before sticking his head out the door and calling for Viper.

When Viper and Razor come to the door, I'm not ashamed Grainger is standing in front of me both as protection from any threat and from any man other than Ace seeing me naked. Viper is quick to take in the room's scene and put the pieces of the puzzle together. Grainger and Viper swap places and Razor comes over next to Viper to help make a wall of muscle to shield me from my uncle Hunter's view.

I watch as Hunter comes into the room and treats our tour guide as best he can with his limited medical supplies for her particular injuries. Plus, he doesn't want to mess with evidence that the police will want.

While Hunter is distracted with his patient, Razor removes the gags and unties the rest of the women. The next bit goes by in a blur, but I'm reunited with Ace and when a paramedic comes in to check on me, I realize I'm shaking like a leaf.

Ace doesn't leave my side the whole time at the hospital, even when the doctor suggests he might not want to hear what happened during our time separated. The doctor understood we had both been held hostage together, but he thought Ace couldn't handle to hear what I had gone through.

He knew at least one woman was raped, and from mine and the other women's states of undress, he had his suspicions about what else had happened. I had come close to being raped, but the man had never penetrated me.

Viper and the rest of the crew show up at the hospital to check on both me and Ace. When we are released they help me into the van and take me back to headquarters. None of the men ask questions about what happened to me, they treat me normal, sort of. It's hard to act normal when you're dressed in clothes given to you by the hospital. I'm exhausted after the hours of testing, followed by the time in captivity and the hospital visit. I can't express how happy I am to be surrounded by the men in my life. Everyone of them is concerned about me, but they are also giving me the space I need. On the way home, I doze off on

Ace's shoulder and no one says anything to me when they wake me up once we are back at headquarters.

My dad even comes over to me and wraps me into a giant bear hug. I can tell he and mom have been crying. No one has told me how N.R.T. got involved in our rescue, but tonight isn't the night to ponder those questions. While I was being examined at the hospital, I had plenty of time to think about going to college in person and I've made my decision and it's a hard no on going to campus for classes. I'll have to find a major that I can complete completely online, so the EMT/paramedic major is out of the picture.

The next few days, I refuse to leave the comfort of my room. Ace tries to console me, but every time I close my eyes, all I see are the men's faces just before they almost raped me. I see the poor tour guide's face as she's lying there on the ground bleeding and crying naked on the floor.

Ace makes sure I take the medication the doctors at the hospital gave me. I'm not even sure what they are for, but there's a lot of them and I feel nauseous every time I take them. I just want to curl up and sleep, but when I sleep, I'm haunted with nightmares.

Mom and Cynthia come and sit with me to let Ace take care of himself and bring us up some food. They try to get me to eat my favorite foods, but they even make me nauseous.

It's been about a week, maybe more, I've lost track of time since the attack and mom is visiting with me. She's more visiting with Ace than me, since I rarely interact with her prodding. Her prodding used to rial me up and get us into an argument but, I've gone into a shell, which is rare for a person with my hyperactivity. They're whispering and Ace is on my computer looking up something on the internet. I'm not really paying any attention when he gets up and excuses himself from the room.

Exhaustion must have finally taken over since I didn't notice my mom leave nor Ace come back into the room. He's sitting in his office chair next to our bed, just watching me sleep. He looks sleepy himself; I wonder when he slept last.

Chapter 27: Ace

Those fuckers better be lucky they were in custody. It's been almost two full weeks of watching Joanie recover from what they did to her. Yeah, I was a hostage too, but her time with them was worse than mine. When I'd walked into the room where the women were being held, my own brothers were trying to shield her from my view. Her clothes were on the floor and by the looks at the way the other women were dressed, or lack thereof and the woman Hunter was treating, I could figure out what was happening in here to them.

I've watched as she's tried to sleep, only to wake up an hour later sobbing and screaming. The things she saw no one should have been witness to, nor should they be a victim of. To top things off, even though she was adamant about the man never penetrating her, the doctor put her on a preventive medication for antiretrovirals.

He'd explained to me while Joanie was out of it. Even if the man didn't penetrate her but wasn't wearing a condom and had recently had unprotected sex with another person, there was a very miniscule chance that if he, or the person he'd just had sex with carried any std or sti she needed to take the medication.

The medication has made her nauseous from the time she started taking it. At the hospital, they'd run several blood tests to get her preliminary levels. I'd informed the doctor we never used protection and questioned if the medication was safe, if she was pregnant or got pregnant around the same time. He'd questioned me about when we'd had sex and I'd been honest, we'd had sex the night before. I knew it was too early to detect a pregnancy, but he assured me that if she was pregnant, it wouldn't affect the baby.

For almost two weeks, I've been feeding her clear liquids and holding her when the nightmares come. When she'd dozed off on her mom today while I'm on the computer, I use the opportunity to slip out and head down to the security room. The police returned our phones the other day, but I haven't been able to go and retrieve them from the security office. While I'm there, I've got some snooping to do.

"Hey Ace, how is Joanie holding up?" Viper asks, as I step into the security room.

"You know, it's a process. She at least lets me hold her." Viper nods at what I've said. Cynthia took some time to come around before they got their normal back.

He hands me our cellphones, and I work up the nerve to ask him if I can have Hawk or Zeke peek at Joanie's medical records.

"What are you looking for? I don't want you prying into her mental health stuff." He states.

"It's not got to do with that. I've been researching the side effects of the medication the doctor gave her, and her side effects are more pronounced than they say she should have." I try to explain.

"Okay, but no peeking into mental health. You two hear me?"

"Yes, sir," Zeke and Hawk say in unison.

"I'd love to stay and see what you find out, but I've got to balance the books. I really need to hire an accountant, but that's something for another day." Viper says as he heads into his office.

"So, bro, what are we to be looking at in Joanie's medical records?" Hawk asks me.

"Blood work results." I say shortly I'm not about to give to them anymore information to gossip about until I have proof.

Zeke and Hawk click away, hacking into the hospital's records system. One writes the code to cover their tracks while the other hacks and finds the information that I've requested.

"Okay, I'm in her records. You want the blood draw they did the other day, right?"

"Yup."

"Give me a minute." Hawk says.

He clicks away and reads the screen as if he's speed reading a book on his computer screen. "Got them. There's four pages of blood tests." He says. "Wait, the doctor ordered one more after her medication was ordered."

I know deep down that's the test I need to see the results for. He'd already ordered the antiretroviral medications before we'd talked about the possibility of pregnancy, and the way the doctors are trained, they're trained to save the mother first, baby last unless they can save both the baby and the mother's lives at the same time.

"Go to the last one ordered." I say, looking over Hawk's shoulder.

He scrolls down the screen to the last page and, just like I'd thought, the doctor had ordered a pregnancy test. I stare at the screen. There are three letters next to the test name. Anyone not working in the medical field might not know what test it is because the test is categorized by the hormones it tests for. I didn't even hear the door to the security office open and close. I feel a presence next to me, but I can't pull my eyes off the screen.

"Who's pregnant?" Hunter's voice comes from next to me.

Without missing a beat, I say, "Joanie." I hadn't realized that it was Hunter when I opened my fat mouth.

"We need to get out," Zeke says to Hawk.

I figure someone has realized they have a hacker in the system, but as I stand up, there's a heavy hand on my shoulder. It's not Hunter's hand, it's Ghost and he's pulling me by the collar of my shirt out of the security office into Viper's office.

Oh shit. I'm thinking as Viper stands from his desk, seeing Ghost pulling me into his office.

"What now?" Viper asks, sounding unenthused as we've interrupted his balancing of the books again.

"Get the Jaeger, Viper." Ghost says.

"What? Did I miss something?" Viper asks, the confusion showing on his face.

"Yup, I'm going to be a grandfather!" Ghost announces, sticking his chest out further than I thought he could. He's proud I've knocked up his daughter, WTF.

"Really? Ace?" Viper asks as he grabs the green bottle of the horrid tasting liquor and three shot glasses.

"Nu uh. Get this fellow a whiskey glass. It's the last time he's going to be able to get his ass drunk before the baby comes." Ghost tells Viper.

Viper complies and hands the ice cold bottle over to Ghost to pour my 'shot' of the vile liquid. I hate that stuff in the shots and now Ghost is going to make me prove my worth to him. Ghost pours a good amount of the liquid into the glass and places it before me. I'm going to be fucked when I go up to the room later.

"I'm going to have to put a stop to you guys knocking up your women. I can't build houses fast enough." Viper says as he downs his shot of Jaeger.

Ghost chuckles and says, "I think Annie and I can give our place to my daughter and son-in-law for their growing family."

Talk about a shotgun wedding. Hell, I wasn't even present for the wedding. I grab the glass of Jaeger and take a sip of the liquid. The first sip hits me like normal. I grimace at the awful taste. It warms my lungs and stomach as it goes down. However, the more I drink, the less I notice the awful taste.

Viper and Ghost continue to talk about me and Joanie as a married couple. In my mind, I'm trying to figure out how I'm going to tell her the nausea isn't totally from the medications, the medications only enhanced the nausea. I don't see Ghost refill my glass, or I didn't care because I know this isn't going to go over the way I plan it when Joanie finds out.

Hell, Ghost is happy about me knocking up his daughter, I'm concerned. But as the drinks keep flowing, I don't care. He's happy and so am I. I'm about to be a father. That should scare the shit out of me, but it doesn't. At least, not in my inebriated state.

When I finish my glass of Jaeger, I stand up and the buzz really hits me. I don't remember going up to my room, but when I wake up, I'm in my office chair and Joanie is sleeping soundly. Annie isn't there. All I can figure is that Ghost and Viper helped me to my room and had Annie leave to tell her the good news.

I watch as Joanie wakes up. She's so beautiful. Joanie smiles at me. I stand up and make my way over to the bed. I slide into the bed behind her and wrap my arms around her. I run my fingers through her hair as I prepare to tell her the news.

"Babe." I say as I place a kiss on the sweet spot of her neck.

"Yeah?"

We've agreed to not have sex until she is off the medication, as recommended by her doctor.

"I think I have some news that might put bring some light to your darkness." I say. I know I'm talking in riddles, but I need her to be invested in the conversation or else she might miss this important news.

"What could that be?"

"Well, you remember when we first met how you said you wouldn't chop these beautiful things off?" I emphasize what I'm saying by giving one of her breasts a gentle squeeze.

"Ow."

"Are they tender?"

"Well, that hurt you caveman."

"When did you notice the sensitivity?"

"When that man squeezed them. But I thought it was because he was intending to..." She pauses for a moment. "What are you trying to say?"

"I think you've put it together." I smile as she rolls over to face me.

"How'd you find out without a test?"

"Well, Jo, I'm a medic, remember. And your symptoms weren't matching up to the symptoms of the medication the doctors gave you." I explain.

"But you still need a test to prove it. My boobs could just be tender." She argues with me.

"Oh, the doctor did one at the hospital when I asked if the medication would affect a pregnancy." I explain.

"So the doctor told you?" I can see the confusion on her face.

"Not really. I had a hunch and had Hawk and Zeke hack into the hospital's medical records." I put my hand up in defense, as she's been through mental health in the past and I didn't want her to think I went poking around in her medical records for everything. "We only looked at the blood work for the other day. And I was the only one in the room who knew what the test was."

"I still don't like that y'all go snooping like that. My dad is sooo. going to kill us."

"Well, about that..." I trail off and smile at Joanie.

"He knows! What the fuck you told my parents!"

"Shh. I didn't intend to tell your dad. I was overcome with happiness when Hunter asked who was pregnant, I told him it was you. I didn't know your dad was in the room, too."

She chuckles at what I've said, knowing her uncle Hunter and her dad. "What'd they do?"

I explain about her dad taking me to Viper's office and getting me drunk in celebration of making him a grandfather. The smile lights up her face and I can see the woman I fell in love with again peeking through.

"Oh, and by the way, your dad married us."

"What!"

"He said he's giving us his and your mom's place for our expanding family. Actually, he said he's giving his daughter and son-in-law the place."

Joanie bust out laughing. "Well, husband, how does it feel to be married?"

"I don't know yet. But I definitely want to put a ring on that finger." I tell her as I begin kissing her lips and pushing her back onto the bed. We might not be able to have physical sex, but we are going to celebrate this moment together.

Chapter 28: Joanie

Ace's hand slides between my legs and his fingers strum on my clit. My mind is still processing the information he'd just given me, but the pleasure he was giving me I couldn't focus on the information. My focus was now on what he was doing to me. His fingers gently stroked over my southern lips and my arousal floods my channel with this bare touch.

Ace hasn't attempted to have any kind of sexual touch with me since our time as hostages. He'd heard about the attempted rape and I feel he was trying to give me time to recover. However, with the excitement of the news, he couldn't keep his hands off me today. My body responded to his touch, as if nothing had happened.

He continues his gentle stroke on the outer lips, continuing to drive me nuts. Slowly, he spreads them and dips a finger inside my channel.

"Have you missed me, baby?" He plants a kiss just below my earlobe, which sends another wave of arousal through my body.

I can't even form words at this moment, even though I try. My legs open wider, wanting more of the attention from him, and Ace doesn't disappoint. He adds another finger to my channel and starts slowly moving them in and out while keeping the pressure on my clit.

Before I know it, I'm feeling the ecstasy that only Ace can bring me. I can feel myself tightening around his fingers. He stills his fingers, but continues his gentle assault on my clit, allowing me to ride the wave of my orgasm.

Ace pulls his fingers out of me and cuddles up to me, where we fall asleep. I can tell he's still got a bit of a buzz from the celebration with my dad and Viper. But that's okay with me, I'll let him sleep it off.

When I wake a bit later, I listen as Ace continues to snore softly. I go over the million questions in my mind. Yeah, the medication doesn't coincide with my nausea, but is Ace telling me I'm pregnant to keep me from getting too depressed about everything that happened the other week? Only he and Hunter saw the test results, and anyone can hack into the medical records and alter them. So maybe he had Hawk and Zeke hack into my records to change the test.

I can't believe I'm doubting what Ace has told me, but men have lied to me in the past and I don't trust things I don't see. What about my tender breasts? Well, the fact I'm about to start my period could explain the increased tenderness. But as I ponder how long they've been tender, it's not my normal. They've been sensitive since around the time we were held hostage. Usually if my boobs are tender, they're tender for a few days before my period, but it usually stops with my period beginning.

I need to get proof. I can't just believe that I'm pregnant on the word of someone. Sliding out of bed, I find an outfit that is appropriate for the warm August weather. It will be the first time since being taken hostage that I'm leaving headquarters and I know Viper, my dad, and Ace aren't about to let me leave without someone with me. So I head downstairs once I'm dressed and have my phone and the credit card Ace loaned to me to get the things I needed for our date before my graduation. He'd never asked for it back, so I'll just borrow a few bucks for the pregnancy test.

Downstairs I find both Taze and Grainger hanging out in the common area. I'm trying to convince one or both of them to take me to town.

"Why do you need to go to town?" Grainger asks as he chews on a toothpick.

"I just need to run to the pharmacy for some things. It'll be a quick in and out, I promise." I answer, looking between the two men.

"I'm not sure. Ace would kill us if we took you and he didn't know where you were at." Taze speaks up as he fidgets on his phone.

"C'mon, he's asleep. Viper is with Cynthia at the doctor's office, and I have no clue where my parents are. I seriously need to go to the pharmacy." I think I'm getting through to these two hard heads.

"Umm. I'm not sure, still Ace will kill us if he thinks we laid a hand on you." Grainger is still mulling the consequences of his actions, flipping the toothpick back and forth in his mouth.

I'm about to beg these to men to take me to the pharmacy when I see my dad and mom walking up with their arms full of bags. Dad has a grin on his face a mile wide.

"Hey there Joanie. You feeling okay?" My mom asks me.

"Yeah, I want to prove to Ace he's got a crazy notion in his head. And neither of these two hardheads will drive me where I need to go." I cross my arms across my chest.

"No, they're smart men. You never take another man's woman anywhere without him knowing, unless he's away," Dad informs me.

"But I need to go to town and Viper is with Cynthia, and you and mom were nowhere to be found. Plus, Ace is asleep in our room sleeping off his buzz. Since y'all partied with him like y'all were still kids. Anyway, he will argue I don't need the items." I tell my parents in more of a bratty child way than an adult way. I'm not really mad that my dad got Ace drunk, but I can't leave without telling him where I'm going and he's passed out in bed, it makes absolutely no sense to me.

"Let me guess, you wanted to go to the pharmacy to prove to Ace you're not pregnant?" Mom asks as she hands Grainger all but one bag she's carrying.

I nod at her question and reply, "Yeah. Why?"

She reaches into the bag she's still holding and pulls out three pregnancy tests. "I figured you would. You are so much like me. I wouldn't have believed the doctors when they told me I was pregnant with you, except they had an ultrasound to prove it." She smiles at me. Knowing me too well. She says, "So which one do you want to take? I got a digital one, one that gives you a positive or negative sign and I got one that uses one line for negative and two for positive." She's looking at the three boxes, studying them and not really paying me any attention.

I must really be turning red because I hear my dad say, "Annie, you're embarrassing her in front of the other men. Just give her the tests and she can go take one and prove it to herself."

"Sorry." My mom says as she hands me all three boxes. It's not going to be a secret long, if I'm pregnant because Taze and Granger are just staring at me, having watched the whole interaction between me and my mom. The rumor will get through the whole group of men before I know for sure I'm pregnant.

I head back upstairs and to my room, wanting to hide away for the next week before emerging again. At this point, at least five men know about me being pregnant, and it will be hard to stop the rest from finding out if I'm not.

I've locked myself in the bathroom with several bottles of water and the three tests mom bought for me. I've read the directions on all three. I can take all three at any time of the day, but the digital has the best odds of not being read wrong. It's foolproof. I can't tell how long I've been locked in the bathroom when I finally get the urge to pee. I decide I'll take all three at once and see if they all agree.

Placing the tests on the counter once I've peed on them, I set a timer on my phone and stare at it. All the tests say they need at least three minutes to show results, but to wait at least five minutes. The timer has only ticked down two of the five minutes when I hear Ace gently knock on the door.

"Babe, are you okay in there?" He jiggles the handle to find I've locked him out. "Jo?" His voice has the inflection of panic in it.

I stand to move toward the door and let him into the bathroom. That's when I notice the digital test isn't saying processing anymore, it's got a result. I debate for a moment to look at the result or wait for the other two tests when I hear Ace knock again. This time it's a little louder. *He's worried I'd better let him in.*

Deciding to let Ace in before he tears the door down and then I'll look at the tests, I unlock the door and open it for him. He wraps me in his arms and says, "Jo, I was worried about you locking yourself in here. What are you doing?" His eyes study me with concern until something catches his eye.

He glances to the counter and smiles as he sees his answer to his question. "You didn't believe me?"

"It's not that, people can hack into the records and edit them all the time. People's blood work gets misfiled all the time. I needed to see the proof." I answer him.

He puts his thumb and forefinger on my chin and tilts my head to looking up at him. His lips gently press against mine and I can't help the flood of heat between my legs. Before I realize it, Ace has pushed me up against the wall by the counter and he's reaching down to grab up one test.

"Is this the proof you need? Or do you need more?" He's holding the digital test up and right there on the screen it says 'pregnant'. I read it several times looking for the word NOT only not to find it.

He picks up the other two and shows them both to me and by gosh, they're both positive. "I really am pregnant." It's more of a statement to myself than to him, but he nods his head and we kiss.

"I was concerned about the medication the doctor was putting you on and there being a possibility of you being pregnant." He explains why the test was run. "We had a discussion about our sex life and the lack of us using condoms. The doctor reassured me the medication wouldn't hurt the fetus."

His hand lands on my belly and I can't help the happiness that overcomes me. I'm pregnant! I'm with a man who cares about me and understands my issues, and I think I've proven to everyone here I'm willing to work hard and put in my two cents.

"I love you." Ace whispers against my neck before he kisses my lips again. It's a gentle kiss, but it still affects me, making me feel a slight buzz from the kiss.

"Ace, you really don't know what you're getting into with the whole baby thing." I say, pushing lightly on his chest.

"What do you mean?"

"My mom. You think she's normal. She's not."

"How?" He's looking at me with that handsome but questioning look.

I motion for us to go into the main room where we can sit and talk, or cuddle and talk. He follows me into our main room and I sit down on the edge of the bed. He sits behind me and wrapping me up in his arms. I could sit like this all day. It makes me feel so protected.

"Now explain how is your mom not normal." He whispers into my ear as he holds me.

"Well, she acts normal around most people. That's until she gets to know you, or if you're family. Then her crazy side starts showing."

"Um hmm." He nuzzles into my neck as I continue. "What kind of crazy are we talking? Little green alien men invading? Or does she hear voices?" He asks me, his voice vibrating against my neck.

"She's an author. She hears voices of her characters." I turn in his arms. "She gives stuffies and animals voices." I want to see the reaction on his face.

"Haven't you heard of Scooby?" He asks just before he does his own imitation of Scooby Doo.

"Yeah, but that character was made for kids to enjoy in a cartoon. Hers have random spats and talk shit to you. It's embarrassing."

"Ahh. I get it now, since she created a character for you, it was fun and games, but once the characters became known to others outside the home, it became a thing to be embarrassed about."

I shrug, it was a bit weird, but it always picked my spirits up. I could laugh and the stuffies could say stuff I wasn't allowed to say as a child. Now looking back after Ace so tore down my mom's craziness, it was kinda normal. Other parents used hand puppets to teach their kids' lessons. She just used what was at hand.

Ace pulls me out of my thoughts when he asks me, "So tell me what kind of things your mom says."

I go into a story about a unicorn stuffed animal I had as a young girl. When I was pretending to teach the unicorn it's English lesson my mom picked her up and said, "Why do I have to do school work I'm a unicorn?" It wasn't her normal voice, it was a totally different voice. Then, as I started to bring my stuffed animals out of my bedroom to where we did our homeschooling, she would use different voices to have them act up. Not wanting to do their own work or hate certain subjects, always similar to mine. Now, as I heard myself talking about it, I realized she was channeling her frustration with what I was doing to show me exactly what I was doing or how to turn hard work and hate into easy work and love.

Chapter 29: Ace

I didn't want to push the subject, but with the security issues I'd seen the morning of her testing, I had already decided I didn't want her going to the college. Then we'd been held hostage, but I didn't know where Joanie stood on going to classes on the campus. Now with the pregnancy test results and her realizing I hadn't been lying to her, I needed to talk to her about what her next move was going to be. Would she still pursue a career in medicine, or would she consider a different degree?

As I sit here listening to her describe how her mom isn't normal, I think back to my life growing up and I wish I had someone who made me laugh like her mom tries to. My mom raised me and my sisters alone, so she was always working, trying to keep a roof over our heads. I never got to see the relaxed side of my mom. I always go to see the worn out mother of three. Personally, I think Annie's quirk is cute and is a way of coping with her life constantly moving around and not having people to talk to her own age.

My fingers trail gently over her back and find their way towards her belly. It's still surreal to me I've put a life in there, and if she thinks I was joking around about putting a ring on her finger, she's got another think coming.

"So, what are your plans for school?" I finally get the nerve up to ask her.

She shrugs as she leans into me and says, "I'm not sure anymore. I wanted to go for medicine, but after what happened, I'm happy with just staying here in my little cocoon. Not that I'm scared to go outside, but you guys are my people and I'm just happy with that, keeping my people near me and not really interacting with strangers too much, other than in the virtual world or over the phone."

"Would you still like to go to college? Maybe do a degree that you could take the courses completely online?"

"What good would a degree do me if I never got a job and used it?" She asks me, looking up at me like I'm crazy.

I shrug my shoulders and say, "You never know, maybe you could get a job with N.R.T."

"Like doing what?"

"Maybe being the accountant, or our personal assistant, or something like that where you don't have to leave the headquarters, or if you do have to leave the headquarters it with 'your people.'" I throw out the idea to her so she can mull over the ideas.

"Are you sure Viper would hire me?" She asks, turning around and facing me.

"I'm pretty sure he needs someone to help him out in the office. He's always overwhelmed with work and now, with Cynthia and the twins coming in a few months, he's going to be even more overwhelmed with everything."

"Hmm. Let me see." She jumps up and gets her laptop.

I watch as she powers it on and cruises the college's website and looks at a few degrees. She really doesn't need a degree to be a personal assistant. She can already type and of the assistants I've seen, the bosses have a particular way they want things to be done, so usually they have to retrain an educated person in the way they want things done.

She spends quite a lot of time looking at accounting degrees. I can see the gears turning and I hope she goes with the degree. It doesn't list much, if anything, that she would have to attend the school for. The elective courses are the only thing she might have to attend the physical school for. But if she plays her cards right, she'd be able to pick electives she could also take online.

"I don't know. I'd still have to go to the college to register, at least for this semester." She says. I know she's feeling it's a bit early for her to go back to the campus.

I drop the subject, not wanting to be pushy. We settle into a comfortable silence. Joanie checks her emails and there is one from the college. They're apologizing for the trauma she endured during her visit to the campus. As I scan the email over her shoulder, they're offering to allow her a full school year tuition free, and they'll allow her to enroll in classes completely online and wave any late enrollment fees.

With the school covering her tuition for the first two semesters, I suggest she takes, her basic education courses to see if college fits her. She opens the attachment file to see her results from her placement testing. Much to her surprise, she scored well on all the tests. She doesn't need any remediation courses in math or English, which makes her happy.

Jo opens several tabs on her computer. The first is the curriculum for a regular university transfer, then she opens a second for a university transfer in business management, both she can transfer to a university. I can appreciate she's focusing on one step at a time. The third tab she opens is for enrollment.

She narrows down her class list to the ones that are for online courses and not already full. She looks and finds an English Composition I course, College Algebra, Introduction to Economics, Introduction to Accounting, and World History. It seems like a heavy load with fifteen credit hours, but I see the logic in her planning. If she gets overwhelmed, she can drop a course and still be considered a full-time student. All courses go toward both the two majors she's looking at, so they'll count to transfer when she graduates and transfers to a university. My Jo isn't wasting her time, she's going to get the most out of the free education.

I know we'll have to go to the college to pick up her books, but I can go with her and we can make it a short trip. Plus, the bookstore is in the main hall right near the security office. I'll carry my sidearm that day and check in with the security office. I'm not going on the campus without it again.

I give Jo a kiss on the top of her head as she finalizes her classes and head downstairs to see what's going on. I've been hearing some noise from people walking by our door as we've been talking. Lord knows what Ghost and Viper have the rest of the guys up to.

I open our door and it's got decorations in blue and pink all over it. With a sign saying 'Guess who's expecting?' There are baby booties hanging around the doorknob. Oh lord, the guys are going all out with Joanie's pregnancy. They've even decorated Viper's door with similar decorations. It's like a sign to the others "don't drink the water or you'll wind up expecting."

I make my way down the stairs with the handrails covered in pink and blue crepe paper and head straight for Viper's office. Once again, he's got his head buried into paperwork. How he manages to get us jobs, take care of Cynthia, and keep the bills paid always astonishes me.

Viper looks up at me for a moment and just grunts. Apparently, the commotion in the main room is driving him crazy. I sit down in the seat across from his desk and clear my throat, giving him time to get to a stopping point. When he looks up again, he motions for me to spill the beans.

"Hey boss, how would you like to have some of the workload taken off your shoulders?" I ask him hoping he's open to the suggestion.

"What are you offering to do?" He almost growls out at me.

"Well, not exactly me. I was talking about Joanie helping you."

"What did she magically get her accounting degree or a management degree?" He's got an attitude today.

"No, but she's looking at doing classes online. Freeing up us men to not have to ferry her to the college except to pick up her books at the beginning of the semester."

He looks at me now, a bit more interested. "That still doesn't solve my accountant problem." He states flatly.

"Well, that's where her major is gearing towards. Its business management or accounting. Those are the two majors she's looking at." I explain to him what she was doing upstairs a few minutes ago.

A grin comes over his face. "So you thought getting some hands on experience would be nice for her?"

I smile back and say, "I only was thinking of helping both you and Joanie. She doesn't want to leave here unless she has to."

His smile turns to concern, and I know immediately what he's about to say. I put my hand up before he voices his concern. "She's not agoraphobic, she just sees us and the headquarters as her cocoon. She'll go out if needed, but I'm pretty sure she'll take one of us with her when she does."

He leans back in his chair, thinking over my proposal. Joanie could do her schoolwork, help in the office, and get hands on experience keeping our books. Of course, he'd have to go over the books periodically, but it would definitely get some of the stress off of him.

Viper finally leans forward after a few minutes of silent thinking. He says, "It's a good idea, but I'm going to pay her what she's worth. Not what you or Ghost want me to pay her."

"I'm fine with that." I say to Viper. "So what's got you in a mood?" I ask.

He huffs out a breath and says, "The appointment today. Cynthia is just now at six months with the first baby and the second is almost there. The doc is concerned about Cynthia's frame supporting the two babies as they grow more."

"But she's hardly showing she's carrying twins." We've been referring to the babies as twins for simplicity. Everyone at headquarters knows the babies aren't really twins, but they will be delivered at the same time.

"Right now. But the first one is about to start really growing, and he's worried the one will push on the second and cause issues with the second's growth." He explains. "I'm worried for my babies and for Cynthia."

"I'm here for you, man. If you need to talk. I feel your pain as Joanie's pregnancy has only started, I'm seeing why you're scared."

We sit and talk for a little while and I see his mood change to a more happy one. I can only hope Joanie helps relieve the pressures of the job from him and I can continue to relieve the stresses of not having anyone to talk to about his concerns with Cynthia and her pregnancy. I leave the office and Viper with his work.

Chapter 30: Joanie

I head out of our room a few minutes after Ace left. My classes are finalizing and I'm to recieve an email about when classes start and when to pick up my books. I find the entire headquarters looks like someone puked pink and blue everywhere. Our door and Viper's door have been decorated with storks, baby booties and paper cut out's of baby cribs, letting everyone know where the pregnant women live.

I know just who is behind this over decorating. My mom. She didn't doubt I was pregnant. She believed it; she knew I would doubt it, that's why she picked up the pregnancy tests. My mom knew I would have to see the positive test before I'd believe something from the hospital that the guys hacked into.

When I get to the bottom of the stairs, I see Cynthia sitting on a couch in the common area and head over to sit with her. She looks at me and smiles. I know someone has told her I'm pregnant. She doesn't say anything, I guess knowing how overwhelming it can be to be the center of everyone's attention.

Cynthia's belly is only starting to show although she's around six months pregnant. I remember when I first arrived here she wasn't pregnant yet. The guys had rescued her and she was trying to gain weight and reacquaint herself with Viper. She'd been held in captivity for over a decade. I don't see myself on the same level of as her. She survived worse treatment for longer than I did. I have been a victim of a horrific incident, but I had my lover with me during the time, she didn't.

I continue to stare, without realizing it, at her belly, when she says, "Are you wondering how your body will handle it?"

I nod. Not realizing that I've been pondering what I'll look like at various times in my pregnancy. Cynthia smiles and says, "The female body is amazing as it stretches to make room for the baby."

My mom comes up behind me and gives me a big hug. She's so happy I've 'settled down' as she puts it. I figured I had been making adult decisions over the last few years was settling down, but with Ace I haven't wanted to really explore things outside the headquarters and the surrounding properties. I guess mom is right, I have settled down. I'm controlling my ADHD more and more and don't really feel the urge to push my limits unless it's with Ace in the bed.

"So, what are we celebrating?" Cynthia asks my mom.

"A little bit of everything. Joanie and Ace's pregnancy announcement, and your and Viper's baby shower."

"Baby shower?" Cynthia says, confused.

"Yes, every woman needs a baby shower, and you're in your last trimester. It's going to get harder to schedule one, especially since twins want to make their appearances earlier than other babies." My mom says, explaining why they're throwing a baby shower for Cynthia now.

"But aren't baby showers usually for the female friends of the mother to be?" Cynthia asks.

I chime in with a piece of knowledge I've gathered over the years. "Actually, that's just an American tradition. In other societies, the men also join in and celebrate the impending birth."

"Oh, I'm sorry. I'd never heard of that." Cynthia explains.

"Its useless information I tend to search up during my school day. It comes in handy from time to time." I shrug.

While the guys are grilling our dinner and chilling out, Annie, Cynthia, and I talk about pregnancy, hormones, and my schooling. They're both happy to hear about the arrangements the school extended to me, and that I'm taking classes completely online. I'm explaining to them about the majors I'm looking at when I feel Ace walk up behind me.

He joins our conversation, but he's got a shit-eating grin plastered on his face. I wonder what he's hiding, but before I can ask him the question, I see Viper making his way over to where we are sitting. When he sits down Cynthia asks, "What changed your mood?"

Viper snuggles next to her and pulls her into him and says proudly, "I've been given some help with my work."

We all look at him strangely, except for Ace, who grins. We all knew with my dad joining N.R.T. Viper would have help in deciding on missions and one of the two of them could always be at headquarters to be the man in charge. So it confused us that Viper was only now realizing how much my dad could be of such help.

"What do you mean Ghost has been helping you for months now?" Cynthia asked.

"Yeah, but remember, I was looking through applications for accountants?" He asked her.

Now it clicked with me why Ace was now grinning.

"So you found someone you want to hire? Who are they, and when will they be able to start?" Cynthia is so overcome with joy she's spouting questions faster than he can answer.

Viper chuckles and says, "Well, I haven't offered her the position yet. But as for when she could start, tomorrow would be nice, but I guess I could wait until Monday."

"So, you're hiring a woman? Do I need to be worried?" Cynthia teases. "Who is she?"

Viper pins me with a look and leans forward. He clears his throat and says, "I don't want to say her name because I haven't offered her the position yet and I don't want to jinx myself. Although I have from a reliable source that she will accept the position I'm offering."

I must have been physically vibrating because I feel Ace's muscular arm wrap around me and pull me in tighter. I couldn't hold my excitement any longer and I blurt out, "I'll take it."

Viper and Ace both chuckle at my sudden outburst. My mom and Cynthia both look at me and the smiles on their faces grow.

"Well, I guess the cat's outta the bag now." Viper chuckles as he extends a hand to shake mine.

Mom and Cynthia bombard me with questions since I knew about the job before Viper said much. I explain about the college paying for a year's worth of schooling and the majors I'm looking into. When I tell them about looking at accounting, it tickled them I'll be able to do my schoolwork and get some hands on experience at the same time.

Our conversation was interrupted by Razor, Hawk, and Wolf coming down the stairs. Their arms are loaded down with wrapped gifts for Cynthia's baby shower, and they are joking with each other. Razor hasn't been able to wear his prosthetic since the day they rescued me from the school, and one captor tore the restraint device that holds it in place. The VA is backlogged, as usual, on replacing prosthetics, so he'll be staying close to the headquarters until he gets his new one.

"There she is!" Beth Ann hollers as she approaches from the garage area. She's got a gift bag on her arm with crepe paper hiding her gifts underneath.

Beth Ann approaches where we are all sitting. While she's hugging on Cynthia, I notice out of the corner of my eye that Razor is hurrying up Wolf and Hawk by dumping his gifts off on them and making a beeline for his room. He's hiding out away from Beth Ann. I knew he had a thing about feeling self conscious about his missing arm, but this is the first time I've really seen him go and hide out to keep from being seen without his arm on.

"Damn, I wanted to say hi to Razor. Do you think he'll come back soon?"

We all shrugged. No one knew how long he would hideaway. He might make an appearance later for food or beer, or he might stay locked up in his room for the rest of the night. No one exactly knows Razor's thinking these days.

I was finally realizing why these guys were my kind of people. We were all hiding away from some kind of trauma. Viper and Cynthia were both dealing with her kidnapping. Ace was dealing with his PTSD and I was dealing with my ADHD and ODD. Razor was dealing with the loss of his arm. The other men I still hadn't figured out what they were dealing with, but I knew they were dealing with things.

"Is he ashamed that he's got a prosthetic?" Beth Ann queries.

"Maybe? I mean, really, who knows what men think?" I supply.

"Who knows what anyone thinks?" My mom says.

I know what she's getting at. She's wondering what's motivated me my whole life. I decide tonight it's time to clear up at least one of those things that she's been wondering what I was thinking.

"I was about to join the Navy." I blurt out.

My mom looks at me, shocked by my confession. As do Viper and Cynthia. Ace isn't surprised since I confessed it to him in the hotel that night. Both Viper and my mom look at him and say in unison, "You knew?"

Ace only shrugs and says, "She told me in confidence. I promised her in the hotel room that night not to tell anyone, and I take my promises to heart." Ace says as he urges me to continue telling my mom my story.

"You mean when she walked in on you in the shower?" My mom asks.

Ace nods, confirming where the conversation took place. "She walked in while I was in the shower, and as the team medic, I was concerned about her mental health. I asked questions to assess her and she just opened up to me. I never betray the confidence of things told to me during a medical assessment."

My dad, seeing the way the conversation has changed, walks over just before I start from the beginning of my story. I tell everyone surrounding me about how my best friend and I planned on joining the Navy on the Friday of a sleepover. How we had kept the secret from my parents knowing that they would be against my decision. I even tell them how the doctor waited until the end to deny my joining the military on the basis of my neurological conditions. I told them how I'd been truthful with my recruiter about my conditions, and the recruiters had informed the doctors at MEPS about it, with the doctors clearing me to come in for a physical.

When I get to the part about storming out and walking down the highway, that's when my mom interrupts me. She says, "That's why you were where you were when Cowboy found you."

I nod. I knew the area and knew I'd be fine. But when Uncle Cowboy had found me wandering near the base, his protective nature had kicked in and he'd ordered me into his car and taken me to my mom. The rest of the story my parents already knew.

Chapter 31: Ace

After Jo had spilled the beans on what she had been up to all those months ago, the party for Cynthia starts. Joanie apologizes to Cynthia for taking the limelight away from her. Though Cynthia isn't a vain woman, she is happy seeing the wound that was separating Jo, Annie, and Ghost mending.

We enjoy a wonderful but subdued party for Cynthia and Viper. Since Cynthia doesn't have many friends outside the headquarters, Annie had invited all of Ghosts' teammates and their wives to help fill out the party. Thankfully, she didn't plan any of the silly pregnancy games most baby showers have. Instead, Annie used it for a chance to break the ice with the wives of the other men and Cynthia.

Annie had cupcakes made for the baby shower and the other women also brought tons of gifts with them. While the women talk and Cynthia opens gifts, the men make sure the women have enough real sustenance to survive on.

Once the party is into full swing, I grab a couple of beers and excuse myself to check on Razor. He's been acting super weird since Beth Ann arrived. I've seen him avoid people in headquarters when he didn't have his prosthetic on, but this is a new level for even him.

I knock on his door and he opens it just enough to peep through and see it's me. I hold up the beer as a peace offering and he opens his door the rest of the way, letting me in. As I enter, he heads over to his bed and flops down.

I open our beers and hand him one. "So what's up? Are you hiding away from Beth Ann?" I ask him as he takes the beer from me.

He shrugs and says, "I don't know. I just don't want her to see me like this." He uses his beer bottle, gyrating wildly at his lack of a lower portion of arm.

"You know she knows you wear a prosthesis?"

"Yeah, but I look like a freak without it."

I lean up against his bar and smile as I take a sip of my beer and contemplate what he's said. None of the guys at N.R.T. think he's a freak, but it's his view of himself. "Why don't you let her make that decision for herself?"

"What?" He almost chokes on the sip of beer.

I can't help the laugh that escapes from my mouth at his reaction to what I just said.

"Do you think I care what Beth Ann thinks? Do you think I like her or something?" He asks, sitting up on his bed.

"Well, by the way you're acting, I'd say you've got some kind of feelings for her. You've usually stayed in the shadows of headquarters when we have guests here, but today you're totally hiding away since you spotted her." I point out the way he's been acting.

"You and Viper wouldn't understand."

"What wouldn't we understand? And since you only reference me and Viper, I'm assuming you have feelings for Beth Ann. Does your cock not work right?" I tease him a little to get Razor to open up to me.

"No. My cock works just fine." Razor defends himself. "I-it's just that I haven't been with a woman since I lost my arm." He finally admits.

Now I get what he's getting at. He's nervous about attempting sex with only one good arm. "Dude. If you both want it, y'all will figure out a way." I try to console him. "But don't avoid her and lose out on the one person who could have given you the stars."

He seems to contemplate what I've said. We finish our beers and I make my excuse to get back to the party. As I'm getting to the door, Razor says, "Wait, I gotta take a piss and I'll walk down with you." I stop with my hand on the doorknob as Razor goes to the bathroom.

We walk out of his room together and back to the party. I head over to the fridge where the beers are and I grab three more. One for each of us and one for Beth Ann. As I've got my back to the party, I hear Beth Ann squeal, "Razor, I thought you would never come out of your room. Are you feeling okay?"

She's wrapped him up in a hug and as he's straightened up, he's picked her up off the floor. Her legs are bent at the knees, trusting he's got her. Razor has wrapped his one good arm around her back and is tightly holding on to Beth Ann.

When I walk back over with the beers, I hand the two to Razor and Beth Ann and offer to open theirs. Razor not to be emasculated, so he grabbed their beers and opened them using his thighs to hold them as he twisted off the tops.

I'm holding Joanie and watching the interactions between Beth Ann and Razor. I can see the two of them just like Joanie and myself in another year or two. *What the hell has gotten into me? I'm picturing my teammate married with children.*

Joanie leans into me after several hours of baby shower oohing and ahhing over the gifts for the baby and for Cynthia. I can tell she's exhausted. I stand up and clean up the empty beer bottles and plates from the table in front of me, and take them to the trash while Jo says good night to Cynthia, the rest of the guys and, of course, Beth Ann.

As we're heading to our room, Ghost gets up and walks over to where we are. He smiles at me and says, "Nope son, y'all aren't staying in there anymore. I wasn't lying when I said you and Joanie could use the house for yours. Take my daughter and enjoy your first night in a real home."

I hadn't even noticed, but apparently he and some of the other men from his team had moved the bed from my room into the master bedroom of the house that was built for him and Annie.

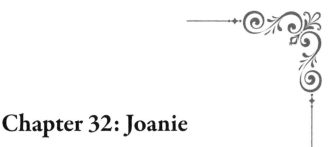

Chapter 32: Joanie

It had been two weeks of nauseating medication when I found out I was pregnant. Ace and I couldn't celebrate properly since the medication had to be taken for six weeks, and I had to be tested again for STDs and STIs at the end of the six weeks. But I have to say Ace is on the ball because he's contacted the doctor that comes to headquarters to do an ultrasound and determine how far along I am.

I am dealing with anger at the men that took us hostage since I can't be intimate with Ace. It annoys the piss out of me. When the doctor comes and does the ultrasound, we find out that I'm six weeks pregnant. I'm due in May. Of course, Ace was there through the whole ultrasound and he's made sure I've taken every one of those horrid antiretroviral pills.

I've been working for Viper since after Cynthia's baby shower. It's been nice to work for him. Viper showed me the ropes of keeping his books and I pretty much got the idea of it and left him alone. To say he was happy to look over the balanced books at the end of the week is an understatement.

I even received an email from the college about starting classes. The school counselor approved of my selected classes and I'm excited to find out that I don't need to purchase any books from the school. All my online courses come with an e-book copy of the books. I can opt to buy a physical copy if I want to but the less I have to step on campus, the better.

Today, Ace and I head out to the hospital. I've finished the antiretroviral medications, and the doctor needs to run bloodwork on me. It's not the kind of bloodwork our normal doctor can do. Plus, we have a baby doctor appointment, as Ace calls my OB appointments. I'm officially nearing the end of my first trimester.

I feel weird heading out to the hospital, because not only is Ace with me, but Razor and Grainger are also going with us. Viper isn't slacking on my security ever again. Grainger stays with the van while Razor escorts Ace and me to the lab. There they draw blood and perform a rapid test, which I have to see the doctor for the results for.

We head as a threesome for the doctor's office where Razor stays outside in the waiting area, giving us some privacy. Thankfully, the OB is the doctor going over the results of my lab work. I anxiously waited for the OB to show up. When she enters the room, she's holding a chart and I can feel my heart rate jump as I want to get the appointment over with and out of this hospital.

"Ms. Anderson, how are you feeling today?"

"Good, I guess."

"That's understandable. You've been through a lot in the past few weeks. I know you're anxious to know the results from the bloodwork. So, let's calm your nerves down and give you the results. Is this your baby's father?"

"Yes." Both Ace and I answer in unison.

"He knows about the medication you've been on and why then, correct?"

"Yes."

"Well, your viral load when you were admitted six weeks ago was zero and it is still zero." She says without addendum.

"Now let's listen to your baby's heartbeat and give you something else positive to leave this appointment with." The doctor pulls out something that looks like a handheld radio with an attached stethoscope. She places it on my abdomen and begins to move it around until the room is filled with a whooshing sound.

"Is that our child?" Ace asks with wonderment in his voice.

"Yes, that's their heartbeat." The doctor answers him.

It's more real now than it was when we first entered the office this morning. It had been I have a baby inside me, yeah right, four weeks ago. I couldn't feel the baby moving like Cynthia can. But now I've heard my child's heartbeat and it's so real. I can't help the tears that slip from my eyes.

As we leave the appointment, I can't help but notice the hand not holding Ace's is resting on my lower abdomen. Almost in a protective nature.

Chapter 33: Joanie

A few days after I got the all clear, my dad, Ghost, informs everyone that in a few weeks we are heading up to Chicago to attend a graduation ceremony. His team is to be the honorees at the ceremony. I figured when he announced the date at the end of September, it would coincide with Liam's graduation.

When school started, it wasn't hard for me to settle into the online college setting. I had done online schooling for my entire life. The school didn't have any kind of virtual class connects, they only had threads you had to post to showing your understanding of each week's topics. There was also a ton of reading to do, but it's nothing I'm not used to.

When the end of September has rolled around, mom and dad remind me of our trip to the graduation. It's a whole SEAL team affair. Six SEALs, their immediate families and, well, my boyfriend. It's only a few days out of the safety of the headquarters, but as I'm packing I'm feeling nervous about seeing Liam in his dress blues for the first time. He's in a special division in boot camp, from what Ace has told me. If his contract contained his agreement to be a SEAL, he was put into it from the beginning.

I wonder what Jen is doing in boot camp. She and Liam both left around the same time, but I haven't had the nerve to write her back with everything I've been through in the past few months. She should also be close to graduation, maybe. But I know the way things can go in boot camp, you can fail something a couple of times and be forced back a week in training, or even have a medical issue and be forced back or even discharged.

Wednesday Viper, Damien, and Wolf drive three of their vans loaded down with our families and the luggage. Ace and I are sharing a bag and dad has been nice enough to get us a hotel room together. We take off for Chicago in the afternoon on Wednesday. It's the best time of day to leave for the Chicago area, according to my dad.

The flight from Texas to Chicago is okay. I really don't like planes, and after my attack, I'm noticing I don't like to go places with lots of people. But thankfully, Ace is right by my side through everything. He's holding my hand and talking quietly in my ear. I think our SEAL family has three quarters of the plane, so it makes me a bit more comfortable that I know most everyone onboard.

We arrive late in the evening on Wednesday and just for fun dad and the guys go by the USO area of the airport. We get to watch a group of new recruits herded out to waiting buses. *Man, they look scared shitless.* After seeing the baby-faced recruits, we head to the rental area and pick up the cars the guys rented for our time here. Of course, in typical SEAL style, they rented nothing but black SUVs.

We check into the hotel and unload our baggage. Then head out to dinner. A fancy Italian place in the heart of Chicago. I'm scared to see what the bill looked like, but dad picked up the tab. Of course, the rest of the team tipped the waitress since we were such a large crowd and she did such an awesome job remembering our orders.

Thursday comes and we head over to the base. It's the first time I've ever seen Great Lakes Recruit Training Command in person. I have to admit its awe-inspiring. While dad and the rest of his team meet with the commanding officer of the base to go over their role for tomorrow's graduation, Ace and I walk around the base. He tells me the names of the barracks and that each is named after a ship. He even tells me where his division was at during boot camp; Ship 12 the Seawolf.

As we are talking, he brings me over to where the recruits pass through 'the tunnel' as he puts it and they sing Anchors Aweigh we stand there for a while and thankfully two divisions pass through one after the other trying to outdo each other in their volume inside the tunnel. A third division approaches the tunnel and they are wearing pt gear and carrying seabags I hear Ace mutter, "Those are some sorry chaps."

"Why do you say that?" I ask him.

"Well, it's the end of September now and with boot camp being nine weeks, they will be here until the middle of November. They're going to be lucky to get out of here before the first snow falls." He explains.

"Oh." I reply.

"And if they're not lucky, they'll spend Thanksgiving stuck here." He adds.

"I noticed the new recruits didn't sing while walking through the tunnel. Why?" I ask Ace.

"Simple. They haven't earned the right yet. You see, the first issue of clothing, which is what they have right now, tells me they haven't even learned to march. In a few weeks, they'll come back for what's termed issue one. During it, the RDC will teach them the process of singing the hymn during the tunnel. Most divisions fuck it up royally and get beat for it at issue. By the time they walk through for issue two, they've come through this tunnel so many times they know the hymn by heart and it's almost perfect. But by graduation time, it's their rite to sing it loud and proud." He explains to me not so simply.

The next morning, we wake up early and eat breakfast before heading back to our rooms for the men to dress in their dress blue uniforms. I've seen my dad and his team in thier dress blues several times, but seeing Ace in his is different. He's sexy as hell in them.

We head to Recruit Training Command and park the SUVs where dad was informed to park. There aren't many vehicles in the parking lot yet, but being the family and the members that are the guests of honor means we have to be there early to be seated.

Dad and his men are pulled away from us and shown into a special area while another sailor shows us where we are to sit. I'm thankful that Ace is by my side as well as the rest of my aunts and my mom.

It seems like an eternity, but finally we hear a drumbeat coming down the avenue, and it's getting closer to the graduation hall. The ceremony is about to begin. I'm going to see my brother for the first time in several months.

What appears to be a garage door opens, but only a little. Someone enters and walks up to the reviewing stand. They exchange a few words and a couple of minutes later, the Navy band marches in from a side door.

The graduation ceremony begins with a group of sailors bringing in the state flags and the American flag. Following them is another group of sailors with rifles that perform some close order drill they've learned. As they are performing, we're told these are recruits that are in various stages of training.

Finally, the garage door opens and the parade of recruits march in. It's the first time we get to see them in their uniforms. They've been standing outside the entire time the band, flags and other performing units were doing their performances.

I've been so distracted with what was going on in front of me I didn't see my dad and his men come into the graduation hall and take their seats down in front of the reviewing podium. I'm still trying to find Liam in the crowd of graduating recruits. Each time a division passes in front of the reviewing stand, the first time their uniforms are covered with their pea coats.

Once each division gets to their designated spot, they go through an entire process to remove their pea coats and place them in a spot on the back wall. Today there are twelve graduating divisions. The announcer informs us.

"Divisions five zero five through five one five, division nine one three and division eight one zero. Division nine one three is the performing drill and band division." The announcer pauses, allowing the audience to take in the group of graduating recruits. "Recruits in the eight hundred divisions have specialized contracts that require them to not only master the regular requirements of boot camp but to spend extra time at the pool and rifle ranges."

"Those are the future SEAL, search and rescue, and such." Ace whispers into my ear.

Now I know where Liam is. Somewhere in the group of the graduating eight hundred division.

The graduation ceremony continues with all the pomp and circumstance of any other military ceremony. Prayers, having the flags read off one by one, parading the graduating recruits by the reviewing stand again, and listening to the sailors repeat the sailors' creed and sing the Navy hymn.

It's nearing the end of the ceremony when the announcer says, "We have a special group of guests with us today. Graduating today is Liam Anderson, the son of Commander Jason Anderson. Commander Anderson and his team have protected our country both on foreign soil and here on our own soil. Many of their missions are still classified. My staff and I felt it appropriate to have the men of Commander Anderson's team hand out the awards for today's recruits that have gone above and beyond the call of duty while in boot camp."

As if rehearsed, Dad and my uncles all stand and execute a right face. They take several steps to a marked spot and halt, then perform a left face.

The announcer begins again describing the first award while, as I'm watching, the award is being handed to my dad. The first recruit is announced and smartly falls out of their division, taking measured steps up to my dad. He shakes my dad's hand and receives his award. Both the recipient and my dad perform an about face and head back to where they came from.

The rest of the team, while dad is marching back to his seat, performs a right face, takes one step forward, and then a left face. All the while, the announcer is describing the next award, who donated it and what the recipient that is being awarded this award did in order to get noticed.

This continues for the six men of dad's team. But that's not the end of things. The announcer says, "We have one more surprise up our sleeve today. There is a young lady here in the audience that wanted to be a sailor, just like her father. However, medical didn't approve her. It has come to our attention that while her best friend Jennifer Zimmerman has been here in boot camp," he pauses as I watch my best friend walk up to the podium. "She has been through a time fit to earn the title of a sailor. Joanie Anderson, would you please make your way down to the floor and stand next to your shipmate?"

I get up and start to make my way to the floor next to Jen. The entire time the announcer is telling the crowd, "You see, Joanie is also Commander Anderson's daughter, and after the Navy rejected her enlistment, well, she decided to try going to college. Not only was she held hostage during her admission tour. But, it was what happened a few weeks earlier, her boyfriend, also a former SEAL, and herself were attacked after a meal. He gave her instructions and she began to follow them, however she couldn't leave him to die, so she returned to the scene and throwing all caution to the wind. Commander Anderson's daughter showed the perseverance of any military member. So today her father, Commander Anderson and her best friend Jennifer Zimmerman are presenting her with both an honorary certificate of graduation from Navy boot camp, and The Navy Distinguished Public Service Award, an award from a greatful nation.

I can't believe it. My best friend is giving me a certificate as an honorary graduate of boot camp, and my dad is presenting me with an award for my acts during my time when Ace and I were attacked. I didn't think my actions were that heroic. But I guess the guys must have.

After the ceremony, we get to see Jen for only a few minutes. Her family came up to see her graduation too.

"So, you've been through hell." Jen says.

"Yeah, but I've got a good man with me, and we've got a totally different life planned than I'd ever thought of." I rub my belly, hinting at the news.

Jen squeals. "What did your parents say?"

"Well, dad flipped out at first when he found out we were sleeping in the same bed, but then he chilled out. Mom was chill for the most part the entire time. It was Uncle Hunter and Aunt Skye who tried to kill him. Hunter caught us having sex, and, well, he and Hunter got into it. Skye came out to defend her husband and, well, stabbed Ace in the arm."

"So, where is this Ace?"

I point over to where Ace is casually talking with the captain of the base and several other officers.

"Uh, I'm not walking over there. Just seeing officer stripes makes my gut churn. How can he be so relaxed with the officers?"

"He works side by side with two on a daily basis and he's probably saved their asses a few times."

"Well, I'll have to meet him later. Maybe the next time I visit," Jen says as her parents' approach, wanting to take her off base to visit and celebrate.

Chapter 34: Epilogue: Ace

It's March and Joanie is on spring break from her school. The bluebonnets are starting to bloom in the field just south of where our house is, well, really it's Ghosts' and Annie's house. They're just living in headquarters until we get our place is built. I know how much she loves these flowers and that's why I've chosen to take her on a picnic out here today. Even though she's a good seven months pregnant and doesn't like going far from the bathroom for long she looks so beautiful pregnant with our child.

She's even settled into the job Viper gave her very well. He watched her like a hawk for the first few months, but after the taxes were done and she'd shown him a few tax breaks he'd missed he let her have free reign on the books. Though he looks over them once she's balanced them at the end of every month. He's been much easier to get along since she took over handling the books, and I'm happy about that.

I got up early this morning and got the side by side ready for our little trip to the field. I've packed a blanket for us to sit on, pillows for Joanie to get comfortable with, drinks for both of us, and a picnic lunch. I know it's not the most romantic thing, but I feel it will be for Joanie.

I asked Ghost if I could have her hand in marriage last week when we were working on Hunter's house. It was funny because he said, "I was starting to wonder if I would have to take you to the creek and waterboard you to set you straight." In other words, I have his permission. Now if she only says yes.

Joanie has been in the office all morning working on catching up on the last missions' expenses. I get to hear it from her about how much we spend on a mission, or thereafter. The upkeep of our weapons, clothing, and vehicles is pricey, but necessary. Plus, once a mission is over, we all like to come home to the ladies nice and clean, so we typically splurge on a hotel for a night. It used to be a night for R&R, but since Cynthia and Joanie came into the picture, women are out of the question for Viper and me.

I've got everything packed and my nerves are amping up. I know it's now or never. I just need to go grab Joanie and take her on our lunch 'date'. I head over to her office door and wipe my sweaty palms on my tee shirt. Joanie opens the door and damn, does she look sexy. She's wearing a pair of maternity dark blue capri pants and a cream color button-up shirt that has no sleeves, but the material is a satin like so it's lightweight and allows her body to breathe.

We walk out to the side by side and I help Joanie into her seat before I get in on the driver side. She groans, "Is this safe for the baby?"

"Don't you worry Jo, we're not going far."

She doesn't know Viper and I have been evening out the trail to her favorite place and I've even secured our house to look out over the field of bluebonnets. I want my woman to always remember the field as the place where she'd gone when I admitted my true feelings for her and where I proposed to her.

I drive us at a comfortable speed so not to jostle her or the baby too much. Just as the bluebonnets are coming in sight, I look over and her face lights up. I jump out of the side by side and quickly grab the blanket and pillows, putting them on the ground before I go and collect a giggling Joanie and the basket of food I've prepared for our lunch.

I help ease her down onto the ground and then, once she's comfortable, I sit down with the basket. I pull out two bottles of water. It's what the two of us drink most of the time, and since most of the other drinks are off Joanie's list, I've been drinking water with her. Next, I pull out the container with her favorite fruits. I spent most of the morning chopping and fighting the guys to keep their grubby paws off our fruit.

Joanie smiles when she sees the fruit dish I've made for us. The container is one of the largest ones I could find that had a lid on it. My woman has been eating fruit like it's going crazy since, well, since the beginning of her pregnancy.

I know we can't survive on fruit alone, so I pull out the next container. It's got several sandwiches in it. The doctor gave her a list of foods to avoid and foods that were good for her and the baby. While I've been supportive of her avoiding sodas and other sugary or caffeinated drinks, I can't go without sandwich meat, and that seems to be the doctor's favorite enemy next to fish. I made for her a peanut butter and jelly sandwich, and for me I made a hoagie, loaded down with tomato, lettuce, salt and pepper and as many types of meat as I could get my hands on. Actually, until Annie reminded me Joanie will lose most of the weight when she gives birth while the weight I put on well, it'll stay on.

We eat lunch until we are both full enjoying a beautiful afternoon with a wonderful scenery. As I begin to clean up our empty water bottles, and the empty dishes. I'm placing them in the back of the side by side when I turn around Joanie is watching me. She's not awe-struck by me anymore, but she enjoys watching me do things. Multiple times she's expressed how she wonders how she snagged me. In her words, 'as fucked up as I am, I have to keep pinching myself when I wake up with you. Because I wonder how I snagged you?'

I turn back to the side by side and pretend that I forgot to tie the picnic basket down. When really I'm grabbing the hidden box with the engagement ring in it. I turn back around and Joanie is trying to get up and help me with the blanket and pillows. But she stops when I kneel on one knee.

I pull the box from behind my back and I say, "Joanie, you settled the nightmares that kept me up at night when we first met. Now you're carrying our child and I promised you a while back I wanted to put a ring on that finger. I'm asking you now to make me an honest man. Will you marry me?"

She drops the pillows that are in her hands and her hands fly to her face and the tears stream down her face. Her hands cover her mouth and I can tell I utterly shocked her. Her mouth is moving, but no words are coming out.

"Babe, I need an answer." I prod her.

Instead of answering me, she gets down on her knees and places her hands on either side of my face. Our lips gently graze each other. I keep my lips closed since I'm still waiting on her answer. She peppers my lips with kisses. It's when she pulls back just a little she whispers, "Yes. I'll marry you."

I wrap my arms around her and kiss her like there is no tomorrow. Laying her back down on our blanket, just before I make love to my woman the way she likes me to.

The End

Thank you

Thank you for reading the second book in the No Red Tape series. I hope you enjoyed reading it as much as I enjoyed writing this installment. Keep following these men on their journeys in finding strong women that compliment them. If you haven't already read Viper and loved this one, I encourage you to catch up on how it began for the team to start falling in love, also if you have questions about the characters of Ghost and his team check out my Healing With a SEAL series. Please leave a rate and review if you really enjoyed this book and series.

Feel free to follow me on the following social media sites. Instagram @authorhblack, Facebook @authorhblack, Goodreads and Bookbub.

Also by Heather Black

Healing With a SEAL
Ghost
Hunter
Cowboy
Able
Dutch
Renegade

Love Emerging
The Doctor's Aphrodite

Standalone
Her Sanctuary
Glitter and Polish
Violet's Tangled Web
Bella's Devil Doc
Sapphire
Viper
ACE

Milton Keynes UK
Ingram Content Group UK Ltd.
UKHW011142220424
441551UK00007B/751